Bearly A

Lady

Cassandra Khaw

BEARLY A LADY
Copyright © 2017 Cassandra Khaw

This first edition published 2017 by Book Smugglers Publishing
Astoria (USA) & Cambridge (UK)
www.booksmugglerspub.com

Edited by Ana Grilo & Thea James

978-1-942302-51-3 (Ebook)
978-1-942302-50-6 (Paperback)

Cover Art © by Muna Abdirahman
Cover Design © by Kenda Montgomery

Book Design and Ebook Conversion by Thea James

To Elena, my sister, the undomestic goddess of the high wire.

Prologue

London.
The Big Smoke.

IT'S LATE, AND THE STAR-STARVED sky's a shade of indigo-black. Street lamps keep watch over lonely streets, even as the last drunks waddle unsteadily to the tube, singing Taylor Swift medleys at the top of their lungs. Occasionally, someone will trip and apologize to the cobblestones in a gently peevish manner.

A girl erupts from a bar, trailed by a gaggle of equally ine-briated friends, all female, all inappropriately dressed for the damp London weather.

"Let's go for some curry!" shrieks the first girl, after taking a moment to evaluate the options. There aren't very many.

A triumphant chorus of assent, but then:

"Actually, I could go for a kebab?"

"Wot? Really?" asks the first girl. "After we'd all said curry?"

"Well, *you* said curry," grumbles the dissenter. She's paler than her counterpart, longer-haired, but otherwise indistin-

7

guishable from her sisters-in-booze. "*I* didn't say curry. No one else said curry. We just made noises. I mean, it's really up to you. You did show initiative, but I thought we could do both, you know what I'm saying? Curry and kebab? No one's got a curfew, right?"

"No."

"No."

"Um. Actually, me mom said she'd really prefer it, if I came home early."

That gives the group pause.

"Oh. Sorry. I guess we should have asked."

"No, I'm sorry. I should have said something—"

"Sorry."

"Sorr—eek!"

A girl screams, jumps back, finger thrust at the colossal silhouette barreling down an alley. It's an imposing sight, about seven, maybe eight feet, of wide-shouldered muscle. The thing roars, a sound like the honk of an angry brass instrument, and suddenly everyone is screaming.

The pandemonium continues for about another minute, girl and giant trading ululations before at last the stand-off is broken by:

"Wait. Is that a *bear*?"

And it is. Light coruscates across brown fur, catching in button-black eyes, and palm-long teeth. There is no question. This is irrefutably, inexplicably a bear.

"—why's it got undies on?"

To everyone's surprise, the bear suddenly looks down, and in a voice that sounds entirely too human, declares:

"Bugger."

Chapter One

IT HAPPENED *AGAIN*. GUCCI, VERSACE, Juicy Couture—nothing *ever* holds together during that time of month. I'm almost desperate enough to do Sports Direct next. I mean, it's not exactly high fashion, but they do have that line of pretty lycra sportswear. And sales. Loads of sales. Sales pretty much every damn week. It'd be a cost-effective experiment. Really.

"I told you. Granny undies."

I shoot Zora, my best friend-slash-roommate-slash-childhood-co-conspirator, a cold, hard look. The eviscerated remnants of today's wardrobe (Prada, with a dollop of Calvin Klein) require somber observation, not wisecracking. "I don't think you remember how this works."

"You bloat up once a month?"

Bloat. Urgh. I barely resist shuddering. What an *ugly* word. "It's not *bloat*. It's a full-body transformation of my feminine figure."

"OH. You mean that. See, when normal women say a 'full-body transformation of my feminine figure,' what they mean is they've either gained or lost fifteen pounds. Normal women who don't eat people when they're PMS—"

"I didn't eat anyone!"

At least, I don't think I did. Dimly, I remember a cluster of cooing girls, nervously fondling my pelt. One might have booped my nose. Could I have munched on one? It didn't seem likely.

Zora rolls her eyes, shoulder braced against the doorframe. God, I hate vampires. Four A.M. on a Saturday, and somehow she's still sparkling.

Not literally, of course. But you know what I mean.

"The point is this is awful. Why haven't we told normal people that we exist yet? Why can't we just get along? If the world knew that there were werebears out there, werebear women with needs, then maybe, just maybe, we might be able to get an entire line of clothing made exclusively for the chic shapeshifter, and I wouldn't have to—"

"There is not enough latex in the world to fit over your bear butt."

I clack my jaw shut, indignant. That was below the belt. Even if she is right. Once a month, I put on about three hundred pounds, gain an alarming amount of hair, and spend the night worrying I've eaten someone. Of course, that's nothing compared to the morning after when the clean-up crews come to tell you about all the dodgy bullshit you've been up to, and how much they'll have to adjust your "special taxes."

By the way, these taxes? They're all determined by weight brackets; a legislative travesty, I tell you that. You wouldn't believe how weremice abuse this gross oversight.

And—*okay*. I'm three hundred and *twenty nine* pounds, to be exact, but nothing like round numbers for making a point, right? Besides, even if you're splitting hairs, I'm firmly in the middle of my classification.

Anyway, in retrospect, maybe I *should* give up on designer brands. Upper class society only functions in single digits, so I can't really expect them to be able to cater to the needs of the modern shapeshifter. And there's that whole issue of blood stains.

But what if I just rung up someone in Zara? Tip them off on the existence of a whole new demographic and their cumulative spending power. Ask about pioneering some kind of self-cleaning fabric. I could be executive producer if they take up the idea, or whatever the equivalent is called in the high-street retail industry. It'd have to go through the Ministry of Supernatural Affairs, of course, but I could wait. It'd be so worth it. I—

"Zelda. Zelda? Hello? You still 'linked' to Earth?"

Damn my tree-hugging, video game-loving werebear parents to McDonald's hell. "Lame doesn't even begin to describe—"

"Ableist."

"It's—ugh. Don't say that. You know I don't—I'm sorry. Cultural indoctrination is a monster."

Zora flashes a grin that is all teeth. "As long as you acknowledge your errors, *Paddington*."

"God! Can you not?" I yelp, stomping towards the bathroom door. "Get out!"

It's not fair. Back in high school, Zora was the frumpy one, but now she's the glamorous vampire with legions of glow stick-toting hunks and I'm Winnie the freaking Pooh. My only consolation is the fact I can go wherever I want, and a denial of entry is like a brick wall in Zora's face. (You know, vampires can't go where they're not welcomed, etcetera, etcetera. It makes them amazing housemates, though. They're pathologically incapable of stealing your blackberries.)

I slam the door shut and press my back against the wood, careful to avoid putting too much pressure. My bank account can't take the repair costs.

Sighing, I move back to the mirror and squint at my reflection. Really, it could be worse. The monthly hirsuteness is annoying, but nothing meticulous waxing can't resolve. And I suppose there's the whole stigmatization of perceived fatness too, but fuck them. I can armwrestle that Mountain guy from Game of Thrones. Who needs the acceptance of bigots?

Oh, and there's also the fact the Change does *phenomenal* things to my cleavage. I like that part quite a bit.

"You're an earth goddess," I breathlessly announce to mirror-me, who looks like she isn't really buying that ultra-positive thinking crap, unfortunately. Self-awareness? Okay. Self-delusion. So not.

"Earth goddess," I mutter under my breath, hoping it'd sound less absurd the second time around.

Nope. Still ridiculous.

Grumbling to myself, I reach for my make-up bag (Kate Spade, special edition) and fumble at the zip. After two minutes of failing at what normally would take half a second, I take back what I said earlier. The Change is the *worst*. You have no idea how much you can miss manual dexterity until it's gone.

But werebear eventually triumphs over bag. With a roar of triumph, I grope for the eyebrow tweezer. And miss. *Damn it.* Scowling, I try again and this time I get as far as lifting it an inch from the bag before the tweezer shoots out of my grip and somersaults into the toilet bowl.

Fudge.

Frustration itches under my skin, kindling into something bigger, *wilder*. Like a bushfire, it burns fast. Before I know what's happening, rage is boiling through every molecule of my being.

"No, no, no, no." I moan. But it's too late. The last syllable stretches like taffy, dropping octaves, becoming low and guttural and unmistakably ursine. I barely have time to regret my no-sugar diet (emergency chocolate would be so good right now) before the darkness comes and wrenches me into a chokehold.

"Zelda!"

I jolt upright, wincing, at the sound of my name. Glass tinkles. Somewhere, someone is hammering furiously at the door.

"Zelda!"

Everything aches. The world is a blurred chiaroscuro of strange formations, every shape melting into the next. Everything looks like I'm peering through a curtain of salt water. In the distance, I can hear a vague hissing noise. I knuckle at an eye, and squint, hopefully. As far as I can tell, I'm still in the bathroom. And—

Ah. Crap.

"Zelda! Open the door! Do *not* make me come in there!"

"No!" I wobble onto my feet, wood and bits of mirror crunching as I go. "Don't come in!"

"I heard what you did, Zelda!"

"I—I—I just dropped a few compacts! That's all!"

But Zora refuses to be persuaded. "That's not what it sounded like."

"Well, it is." I continue, looking about desperately for a miracle. It's bad. Apocalyptically bad. The shower head's been snapped clean off, the shower curtain's in tatters, and I'm pretty sure that smell means I tried to mark my territory. Which is probably what Zora's going on about.

Also: *ew*, bear-self. Why?

I relent.

"Okay Something has gone a bit—" what's the best word here? "—wrong, but it's nothing our insurance can't fix."

Maybe.

Thank *God* for London Zoo. You wouldn't believe how easy it is to convince people your home's been vandalized by a ferocious animal when you live this close to captive wildlife. Especially when you've got a vampire roommate.

That said, I, Zelda Joshua Andreas (don't ask) McCartney, maintain that Zora's powers wouldn't work quite as well if we were living in a place like, say, Covent Garden. Mind control is like theatre, you see. You need to set the scene to get anything done.

"You really don't have to," Zora sighs.

"You totally do."

"Zel," Zora begins, leaning forward. "Take it from someone who can actually mind control people. You don't need mood lighting."

"But it helps."

"No, it doesn't."

I curl my fingers around my nutella latte. The cafe we're in is absolutely gorgeous. It has the most precious mix of Scandinavian furniture (IKEA-bought, but they make it look amazing, anyway) and Parisian art (at least, I think it's Parisian) ever, and is just big enough to keep you from feeling guilty about hogging a table all day. "How do you know?"

Zora inhales in that exaggerated way she does before she says something horribly patronizing. I use the lull to scope out our environment. Most of the customers look like they were bought wholesale (fake blonde hair, saleswoman grins, pink tracksuits, matching babies) from the Yummy Mummy factory. Here and there, I see a few laptop-wielding teenagers, hair dyed, faces full of existential angst. There's even a sweet old couple for diversity's sake, but they're irrelevant to my search for eye candy.

"Because I can control minds? *Hello?*"

"But it isn't an exact science, is it? Maybe what you're actually seeing is confirmation bias—"

"Please." She lifts a palm. "Just stop talking."

Zora stirs her cranberry-tomato shake fitfully, tossing furtive glances over each shoulder as she goes. When she's certain no one is watching, she pulls a flask from a pocket and drips a trickle of red fluid into the mix.

I take it as a small victory. Zora never publically indulges in her need for the big B unless she's feeling overwhelmed. And given that she hasn't come back with an eloquent counter, I'm going to guess it's because she can't refute my brilliance. (There's a tiny, tiny chance she's just tired of this conversation, which we may or may not have had many, many times already, but I'll take my early morning triumphs where I can.)

Zora sighs rapturously as she imbibes the scandalous fruit, leaning back in her chair, eyes rolling up just a little. Blood has the same effect on vampires as Ecstasy does on humans from what I've been told. (You ever wonder why modern media's all about glamorous vampires lounging in clubs? That's why. Because they look ridiculous after they've fed.)

Not that *I* would know. No one's tried documenting the effect that recreational chemicals has on werebears because, you know, *bears*. I have a distant cousin who says it's perfectly fine to do drugs, but he's a total koala (I *said* distant cousin) so I doubt he's in the position to comment on what a shot (Dose? Pop? Serving? Whatever) of Ecstasy might do to a Kodiak bear.

Anyway.

"So, are you ever going to ask Jake out?" Zora demands, without a shred of warning.

I splutter latte back into my mug. "What?"

"Jake," Zora repeats, sliding forward again. "When are you going to ask him out?"

My cheeks blaze. Jake. Jacob. Yes. Just like Twilight Jacob. Except infinitely hotter because real world werewolves are primal, physical beings with a take-no-prisoner attitude to sowing their seeds. No mooning (ha-ha) about unless they're hungry for a quick bite.

"I don't know." I drag a finger across the rim of my cup, hoping it'd stir a miracle from the cream. "I have to check my schedule—"

Zora flaps a hand, sniffing. "You don't have a schedule."

"Yes, I do! I'm going out with Shaun from accounting."

"He's *dead*."

19

"No, he's not."

"Okay, he's in the ICU, then. In a coma. Which you caused."

I clack my trap shut.

Real talk: that wasn't my fault. I *told* him to get his hands out of my knickers, but Shaun wouldn't stop pawing at me, and it was very close to the Change. Obviously, things *happened.* Bad things, but most importantly, things that were not my fault.

"There's Tom—"

"Who you think is terrible."

I wince at the memory of Tom hip-thrusting at a lamp-post at 4am in the morning. "Lionel from the cafe down the street?"

"Please."

"Reginald?"

"You left halfway through your first date."

And there goes all my excuses. "I—"

"I suppose there's Janine. Actually, tell you what. If you ask Janine out, I'll completely drop the subject."

I stop, frown, and poke my tongue into the inside of my cheek. Janine's, well, Janine's been a story. A story that could have become my greatest love story, all intelligent conversation, soft skin, and a mutual affection for Greek food. From what I hear, there was mutual interest for a few months. A lot of mutual interest, in fact, but circumstances conspired to keep us apart. In the end, we sort of gave up, and romance fizzled into unresolved tension. We're still friends, though, but like everything in Britain, it's all a bit awkward.

(Not going to deny that I could have tried harder, but that isn't what true love is, is it? True love is circumstantial. True love is serendipity. Eyes meeting across a crowded pub, a right word at the right time, a breath, a kiss, the feeling of everything coming together perfectly, like the stirring finale to a Disney movie. Not going "Oh. Sorry. Didn't realize you were dating someone" for eight bloody weeks.)

"You want a muffin? They do fantastic gluten-free white chocolate muffins here."

I make a big show of digging through my purse, careful to avoid eye contact. There's no way I'm giving Zora the pleasure of knowing she'd touched a nerve. I might still have a small crush on Janine. Just a tiny, perfectly inconsequential crush. Nothing worth mentioning at all.

"*My point is,*" Zora begins, louder than she needs to be, voice slightly strained. "Your dating life is exactly like your choice in breakfast foods: *boring.* I'm *sick* of seeing you at home all the time, holed up with Netflix and a tub of ice-cream."

I shift in my chair, barely keeping my mouth from dripping into a pout. "I only do that during, you know when."

"Which is like two weeks in four for you. Just ask someone out, Paddington. Jake, if you feel like wolf. Janine, if you don't. I don't. Care. What's the worst that could happen?"

That question brings me up short. What's the worst that could happen, really? It's not like I'm worried about him going British werewolf on me. I've seen Jake during the full moon. He's big, but I've got at least one hundred pounds on him. Nothing intimidating at all. Just pure animal hotness.

"He says no?"

"Honestly, *Paddington*." Another extravagant eye-roll. Zora's such a drama queen. "Just go out and ask him before someone else snags him, and he suddenly becomes daddy to a million puppies."

I don't have a comeback. Defeated, I push out of my chair and just *pout* at Zora, who is grinning like the cat who caught a canary made out of custard and Chanel one-offs.

"Muffins?"

"Muffins."

(Thank god for adaptive digestive systems. And thank god for not being a werepanda. Bamboo, I'm told, tastes awful.)

Chapter Two

HERE'S THE LOW DOWN ON Jake and I. We've actually known each other for ages and ages. Jake was the first person I met in primary school, in fact, and even as a gap-toothed kid, he was cute. But then puberty struck, and he rocketed from adorable to magnificent. Every girl within a five-year radius fell for him like navy-skirted dominoes.

Not that he really cared.

More than anything else, Jake loved being a werewolf. For the first two years of high school, he did nothing but practice being a werewolf. Which meant he very quickly acquired an abdomen you could break hearts on and shoulders to carry this girl's most elaborate sexual fantasies.

After that, of course, he did nothing but use said gorgeous, glorious assets. By the time we graduated, there wasn't a girl in school that he hadn't tumbled into bed with. (You didn't hear it from me, but I heard that his family had to call in so many mind wipes, they started asking the crews to Christmas as a token of appreciation.)

Except the supernaturally inclined ones, of course.

Like me.

Here's the thing about shapeshifters. We're all apex predators, at least the ones that survived long enough to become a part of today's immigrant landscape. Wolf, bear, ferret. Even the moose (Mooses? Meese? Whatever) are pretty fierce, from what I hear.

And the problem with *that* is that nature never intended for there to be more than one apex predator in an ecosystem. As you can imagine, it's all a bit tense, especially since there's absolutely no way (or politically correct reason) to police the distribution of shapeshifters. As such, what you end up with is a pack of nervy were-things, jumping at every shadow, and eyeing each other funny. Thank god for the Ministry, the various bureaus, the byzantine agreements that allow for interspecies relationships, human-suprahuman interactions, and well—

Anyway.

Long story short, cross-species romances are rare and occasionally fatal. Antelope and crocodile? Nope. Wolf and dog? Horrible, horrible idea. Wolf and bear could have, in theory, gone somewhere, but we were two genetics-crossed teenagers brimming with youthful hormones, who were also laser-focused on surviving high school, not eating anyone, or being eaten by someone else.

Consequently, we stayed out of each other's ways, exchanging cordial words when we could not. Jake went on to become a zookeeper. I got a temp job in Vogue house, and somehow we ended up living practically adjacent to each other.

Purely by coincidence.

Purely.

Okay, I *might* have had some help from Becky in Sebastian Roche, but it was only fair. Two years ago, Becky made me cover for her after she decided to have a 'trial elopement.' It didn't work out, of course, and she came slinking back with her tail between her legs after about a week. But for seven days, I had to help her pretend she was at a self-improvement retreat, looking for her True Self instead of drinking tequila on the shores of dreary Brighton.

So, she helped me get a place in Kensington. For entirely too cheap. Right next to Jake. Purely by happenstance.

Honest.

"Just knock!" Zora hisses from the safety of our doorway. "We can both smell him. He's obviously in there."

"What if he's with a lady friend?" I babble, clutching my casserole dish like a divine talisman.

"Once again, let me point out the fact that we've got heightened senses. If he was, in fact, doing the lobster kettle with an attractive female, we'd be able to tell."

"Wait. What the hell's a lobster kettle—"

"Look." Zora's voice grows flat. "You're the one who doesn't want to text, tweet, Snapchat, or message him on Facebook. You don't get a say."

"Zora, you know shapeshifters—"

"Yes, yes." She flaps a hand. "All courtship must be conducted with a show of one's ability to supply food. I don't understand why you can't *just ask him to dinner*—"

"It's not the same. Besides, this is a step beyond getting a permit and asking him to bloody hunt for tourists in Picadilly."

"*Zelda.*"

"Sorry, sorry. Didn't mean it like that. Anyway, point is, it's just tradition, and—"

"*Will you just knock on the goddamned door already!*"

Before I can comply, the door swings open, revealing Jake in nothing but a low-hanging towel. I gape. Water drips along the topography of his pectorals, down the tributaries of his washboard abdomen, all the way to the beginnings of an Adonis' belt and—

"Yes?"

"I—" I tear my eyes from his hips. "Casserole?"

Jake blinks, slowly, and cocks a stare at me from under lashes thick as sin. "Casserole?"

I shiver. Who knew a faint Scottish brogue could make a boring word like casserole sound so beautiful? His voice feels like a warm tongue pressed against somewhere private. When I finally find *my* tongue, my voice is a croak. "Yeah. Casserole."

Behind me, I can hear Zora slapping her face.

"Is it for me?" Jake prompts, peering into the corridor. He makes eye contact with Zora over my shoulder and bobs his head curtly in way of greeting. Werewolves and vampires have long, bloody histories, thanks to pop-culture. (Which is why Zora spends so many hours at those Species United meetings. As everyone knows, the only way forward is through co-existence. Or possibly uncivil war. Take your pick.)

"Yes." I say, after another fifteen seconds of constrained panic. "Yes. This is for you. It has peppers, courgettes, lentils, sweet smoked paprika. And lamb brains. Because you are a virile beast who needs his meat."

"I'm sorry. What?"

Damn it, Zelda. "Lamb brains are good for dogs?"

"*Dogs.*"

"I mean canines! Wolves and dogs are canids, right? Ahaha. Ha. Ha." I shuttle looks between Jake and Zora. Neither of them are laughing. In fact, Zora looks like she's about to asphyxiate on shame-by-proxy and Jake is, well. Let's just say I've seen dead trout that looked less aghast. "I should stop talking."

"Thank you—" Jake is the first to break the silence. He smiles stiffly, and curls his hands around the proffered tupperware, fingertips brushing against mine. "—for the casserole, um…"

"Paddington," Zora inserts helpfully.

His eyes raise. "Really?"

"*Zora.*" I hiss.

"Your name's Zora?" Jake drops his gaze once again, face pinching with confusion. "Zora Paddington?"

I'm going to kill her. I'm so going to kill her. I'm going to stake her in the heart, find a necromancer to bring her back, kill her. Then do it all over again. As I contemplate different ways to murder that which is already dead, I feel the cool of Zora's skin and turn in time to see her slinking up to my side, teeth bared in a Cheshire grin. "Actually—"

"Zora."

"—her name is Zelda McCartney. And the whole reason we're standing in this corridor, instead of cuddled up in our respective habitats is because she really, really wants—"

No. Nonono. "*Zora.*"

"—to ask you out to dinner some time." Zora raps the curve of her lower lip. "And possibly do the dirty. But, you know. That's up to you two."

Someone end me now.

"Have we met?" He holds my stare.

To lie or not to lie?

To lie. Definitely. Jake absolutely doesn't need to remember the fashion calamity that was a teenaged Zelda.

"No."

"Mm." He thrums the noise inside his chest. "Sure."

I jolt from my misery at the sound of Jake's agreement, fish-mouthing all the while. "What?"

"I said sure." His smile is like a supernova in my knickers. "Dinner sounds good."

"Ah." I wet my lips, and try to ignore the way his eyes seem to be tracking my tongue's orbit, and the way his towel keeps drifting incrementally lower with every breath.

Focus, Zelda. *Focus.*

"So, this weekend?"

"Sure."

"I'll pick you up?"

Damn it.

"At eight?" I add, hastily, backing up even as Jake and Zora level matching looks of disbelief. "Should I pick you up at eight?"

Jake sweeps his lidded, bedroom stare around the doorway. When he replies, it's softly and slowly, each word a butterfly kiss. "If you like, I guess? You could just come over and knock."

"Yeah." My voice twitches up an octave. "Cool."

"Cool."

"*Cool*," Zora echoes, before she appends a hand to my sleeve and begins dragging me back into our flat. Despite the fact she's practically a twig, Zora's actually stronger than I am, a fact I have empirical evidence (we armwrestle a lot) for.

She slams the door shut behind us, turns, and beams. She's grinning so hard that I can see every single tooth, including the pointy ones that she's normally so embarrassed about.

"I win."

It's like Zora yelled "action." Suddenly, everything is moving in fast-forward. My emotions, Zelda's fizzy, champagne-bubble giggle of triumph, the highlight reel running through my head.

I asked Jake out for a date.

More accurately, Zora asked Jake for a date on my behalf.

But still.

Still!

He said yes.

Oh. Ehm. Gee.

I'm going on a date with Jake.

"Oh, god." I sink onto the carpet and resist the urge to beg for a chew toy. "I'm going on a date with Jake."

Zora, already recovered from her fit of mad ebullience, organizes a scowl. She gives a little sniff. "We already knew that bit. Where's the part where you say 'Thank you, Zora. You're absolutely amazing!' 'Where would I be without my best friend, Zora?' 'I can't thank you enough, Zora?' 'You win everything, Zora?'"

"I'm—" I bite down on a whimper. "What if he didn't actually want to? What if he felt compelled to say yes just because we were both there? What if he's calling up all his friends right now and complaining about how he got emotionally blackmailed into going onto a date with Yogina the Plus-Sized Bear?"

"Firstly," Zora huffs as she glides across our living room to the liquor cabinet. "You're not plus-sized. Well, you are. For a human. But you're also actually quite a small bear."

"You know that could be construed as offensive, right?"

"I'm just trying to make a point. You're the one trying to shut yourself down."

She was right. But also slightly wrong. I'm more of a medium-sized bear, but like my Pilates instructor tells me, numbers are an arbitrary construct, meant to create feelings of inadequacy in the target demographic. What matters is how you actually look.

And I look good.

I think.

Bottles and glasses clink and rattle. "Gin and tonic?"

"Does a bear shit in the woods?"

Zora snorts a laugh, even as she picks out bitters and heart-shaped ice cubes. "*Do* you?"

"It's a pithy—" I flap a hand. "Simile. Metaphor. Analogy. *Thing*."

"Saying, maybe?" Zora pokes a tongue against the side of her cheek, measuring out a careful thimble of Bombay Sapphire for each glass, before doing what she always does: pause, look cross, and then toss in another two servings. "Anyway. Whatever. That's not important. Like I was saying before, secondly, did you *see* the way he was looking at you?"

"Yes?" No.

"He looked like he was going to *eat* you up."

I pause. The memory of Jake's eyes (and the soft, dark tuft of down layered over the skin above his towel) burns through me like a good whiskey. Zora was right. He hadn't looked repulsed. If anything, he had looked *hungry*. Like he wanted to tear me out of my clothes and slam me hard against the wall, sink his teeth into an earlobe and his cock into my—

"Zelda?"

"Hrzzh?"

"What were you thinking?" Zora is holding out a glass expectantly, head canted just so, her hair a perfect waterfall of mirror-sheen black.

I snatch the cocktail from her and take a gulp. True to form, it's mostly gin, with the barest bloom of tonic, just enough to provide counterpoint to the bitters. Eyes streaming, I try a smile.

But Zora doesn't buy it.

"I can *smell* you, you know?" She declares in that singsong tone, all teeth, all mischief, smugness wafting from her smile like the stink of gin.

"Fine," I push down on the thought of Jake, his abs gleaming with sweat, his hip-bones grinding against my ass as he pushes up, up into—"I was thinking about Jake, okay? I was thinking about Jake."

And his hands and his muscled forearms and his pectorals, all taut with power, strong enough to manhandle a werebear at her wildest.

"Hah." Zora quaffs a victory sip as she sinks into our sofa, our one piece of unreasonably expensive piece of Norwegian furniture. (We're still paying installment on that nightmare.) She drapes her arms over the back of it, before crossing long, pale legs and tipping her glass. Gin sloshes onto the carpet (cheap IKEA bargain), but neither of us comment. "Called it."

I take a seat on the overstuffed, paisley-patterned love-seat my grandmother had bequeathed us. It gives a disdainful squeak. "Of *course* you could tell."

Zora sticks out her tongue and winks saucily. Much to my relief, though, she doesn't take the teasing further. Instead, she hoists her glass up and announces:

"To hot animal sex!"

She's so lucky vampires don't need to work to get laid.

"To a good date," I counter.

"To hot. Animal. Sex," Zora repeats, in that tone she uses when disagreement is not an option, the words slurring ever-so-slightly. One of the drawbacks to vampiric metabolism is their utter inability to hold their liquor.

I glance at the door as Zora staggers upright to procure more gin, my pulse speeding alarmingly. Hot animal sex. That didn't sound too bad, did it? That didn't sound too bad at all.

I have a date with Jake.

"To hot animal sex," I concede, finally, breathily and toss my head back, the cocktail glittering down my throat, bright as the promise of paranormal romance.

Chapter Three

"FUCK ME! I NEED A dress."

The revelation hits halfway through lunch, and it comes out way louder than I intended. Not that I planned to actually vocalize that burning need.

Janine tips a Look at me from over her spectacles, while John and Kelly giggle like school children. Oscar's no doubt just leering at me right now, but I continue pretending he doesn't exist. One drunken office party hook-up, and he thinks we're going to shag forever. The nerve of some men.

"Does that mean we're goin' out on a second date then, Zel?"

"No, Oscar. It does not," I roll my eyes and glance sidelong at the lout. He's not bad-looking as far as desk monkeys are concerned. Oscar works out. Sometimes. Even has an interesting tattoo on his bum. But all that alcohol and poor attitude is beginning to win the war against decent genetics.

"So, who you goin' out with then?" He persists, his voice gilded with just the barest hint of jealousy. "What's he do? He got a lot of money, then? A big cock? You—"

"Enough."

He shuts up. Everyone shuts up. When Francesca speaks, everyone listens. Suitably cowed, we all turn to stare as the slim, imposingly sleek older woman sitting at the end of the table raps her cigarette holder against the wood. Her ensemble is magnificent: white jacket, white kimono pants, a sequined halter top that has no business looking so perfect on anyone, and this beautiful, wide-brimmed, two-toned hat for a dollop of '50s va-vavoom.

Nothing store bought. That'd be too gauche. Rumour has it that even Francesca's unmentionables are custom-made by a man in Milan.

"This is a lunch table, Oscar. Not a meat market. Have some class."

I bury my laughter in a forkful of green curry linguine. Zora can't abide by this restaurant, preferring more "authentic" venues, but I'm not quite as fussy. Something about the omnivorous disposition of us ursine types, I suppose.

Besides, anywhere with a revolving dessert menu's got my vote. (Salted egg yolk lava cake sounds like it could just about work.)

"So, is it true?" Janine hisses, after the dust has settled and everyone's gone back to small talk and prodding at their respective lunches. "Are you going on a date?"

I scrunch my face into a moue. "Why does this seem to surprise everyone? Yes, I'm going on a date!"

Oscar glowers at me from across the table.

"He cute then?"

"Gorgeous." The word leaps to my tongue, before I can even consider censoring my enthusiasm. "Like a Greek god."

Janine runs a critical eye over my figure. I'm dressed a bit risqué for the office today, I'll admit. The crop-top velvet dinner jacket barely fits around my cleavage, which I may or may not have highlighted with bronzer, and which may or may not be popping out its bustier because Zora laced me in too tight. Everything else is relatively sedate, though. Kitten heels, a non-descript clutch, and a pencil skirt in the style of Francesca Bartonelli.

What can I say? My boss is totally my style icon.

Unexpectedly, a frisson of embarrassment shivers down my spine, and I blush, suddenly self-conscious. I fold my arms over my chest, duck my head, and look away, praying that Janine'd turn her attention elsewhere too. Thankfully, she takes the cue, and moves her eyes elsewhere.

But then she leans forward and smiles at me. "Sooooo. Tell me more."

My cheeks warm further.

"How about I tell you *after* I've had my first date? No need to jinx it."

She makes a big show of evaluating my offer, a loud hmmmm vibrating in her chest. Janine looks absolutely stunning today. Minimal makeup, long dark hair pulled back, pant suit like something Kate Winslet'd wear for the front page of Vogue, monochrome palette setting off the gold in her eyes.

I don't know why she's asking, to be honest. Especially given our history. There's a part of me that's hoping that it's because she's just a wee bit jealous, but I'm not holding my breath.

In the end, Janine accepts my proposal with a vehement nod, and an outstretched hand.

"Fair enough. But I expect details if you two shack up. *Details.*" She grazes a finger up my wrist.

I shiver. "Absolutely."

With any luck, Janine will have forgotten entirely about this arrangement by this time tomorrow.

"*Juicy* details."

"Okay! Geez." *Definitely* time to meditate on a diversion. Maybe, Zora'll lend a hand. Actually, no. I don't want Zora giving me a hand with anything ever again. Especially not with Janine. With my luck, the two will gang up against me instead.

That, and I don't want to risk Zora trying to set me up with Janine, because my heart will absolutely break if I had to listen to any romantic misadventures. I mean, I know we're not meant to be, but it'd still rankle, you know? Just a tiny, tiny bit.

"I want a full inventory of positions, toys, kinky misdemeanors, and choice excerpts from any and all dirty talk that you two participate in."

"That's com—I, wha—*Janine*! Why?!"

"Mostly because I want to see Oscar foam at the mouth," Janine declares with a sideway jerk of her head, chandelier earrings tinkling.

"Oh."

"Also because I'm nosy," Janine winks and I feel a jolt of electricity spasm through me. Let's be clear here. My sexual preferences aren't gender agnostic, per se. On a Kinsey scale, I'd be a 4, or whatever number's the one that's mostly heterosexual but open to opportunities, but there's just something about Janine that makes me go to pieces.

I don't get a chance to ponder my reaction, however. Smiling breezily, Janine switches her attention back to Carol from Human Resources, who is, as far as I can tell, apparently involved in an accidental affair with the owner of a young start-up. These lunches are weird, but Francesca keeps insisting on them. Something about the texture of team spirit.

"How was I supposed to know he's already married—" She moans dramatically, wringing many-ringed fingers, and I'm about to lean into that conversation when:

"Zelda, was it?"

I jump at the sound of Francesca's voice.

"Mrs Bartonelli! I—"

"*Miss*," Francesca corrects as she takes a luxurious pull from her cigarette, suddenly much closer than I remember.

"Oh, god. Sorry. I meant *Miss* Bartonelli. Honest. Freudian slip, I swear. I'm so—" In my panic to stand up, I crash into the table, nearly overturning everyone's half-eaten lunch.

"Sit."

I plunk back down like a repentant child.

Francesca inhales another lungful of smoke. Then, she sighs. A tiny, disappointed schoolmarm noise, full of judgment and mild disdain.

"I've heard a bit about you."

Not a lot. Just a bit. Because that's exactly the kind of woman that Francesca is. If the Queen walked up to her, she'd probably say something like "I've read an article about you once."

"Good things, I hope?"

"Mm." She taps the ash from her cigarette, sighs again, with slightly more gusto this time. "Walk with me."

Without waiting for agreement, the older woman pivots on a four-inch stiletto heel and begins sashaying into the bustle of the restaurant, trailing smoke like a war banner.

Francesca is astonishingly spry for her age. So spry, in fact, that I actually lose her in the din of waiters and high street diners. I'm on the verge of skulking back to the table when I spot her silhouette in a doorway.

She's talking to someone in one of the restaurant's private rooms. I can't quite make out who it is. A man, definitely, lithe and lean, poised as a military officer, his skin pale and almost luminous. His ash-blonde hair is metrosexual-long, salon-fresh, and somehow completely not effeminate.

"Ms.—" I'm careful this time to stress the appellative as I inch into the field of hearing, head slightly stooped. "—Bartonelli? You wanted to talk to me?"

They both turn and my breath hitches. Francesca's companion is beautiful. No. *Gorgeous.* Elegant, lordly. Like something out of a fairy tale or that Lord of the Rings extravaganza. The Desmond Merrion original he's wearing, steel-colored and overlaid with a subtle houndstooth pattern, doesn't hurt the image either.

Or the glamour that clings to him like an attar of perfect honeymoons. I blink.

"Hi."

I can almost hear Bach rising in the background.

His mouth lifts into a smirk. "Hello."

"This is—" Francesca purses her lips before sliding a slim black cigarette free of its gold-bordered case. Wordlessly, he leans forward to light the tip, the small flame anointing his cufflinks in gold. "—Benedict."

I wait.

"Just Benedict?"

"Yes," Francesca sighs again, softly, the cigarette evaporating into a blue shimmer. "*Just* Benedict. I don't need you going into teenage hysterics about Benedict's parentage. Or mine, for that matter."

Realization dawns. Heat runnels into my cheeks and my fingertips, a wash of heat that makes the air a little harder to breathe. That otherworldly sense of fashion. The weird arrangement that Francesca has with the various designer labels. All of it. It now makes sense.

They're fae.

I've been working for one of the Fair Ones.

"I—"

"In case that wasn't obvious, Miss McCartney, that was a subtly veiled order to not fuck. Up." Francesca exhales a regretful plume of smoke. "Frankly, you're my last choice in bodyguards—"

Wait. What?

"—but Benedict *insisted* that I find someone with—" Another long-suffering sigh. "—*curves*."

Anticipation drains into slow, controlled panic. Benedict's just smiling now, hands behind the small of his back, clearly delighted with the proceedings.

"I—"

"And you were the only werebear I could find on short notice with a H-cup."

What.

This is going too fast. I haven't even come down from the high of that unexpected epiphany.

"As such, you are now in charge of my nephew's personal safety while he gallivants through London. Fail and you're fired."

"But I've never even taken an MMA class. I can't fight. I don't even own pepper spray! I'm not—"

"*I suggest you make a few important life changes, then.* And quickly. Because the Sidhe Court will you have your *head* if any harm befalls their prince."

My mouth hangs open. "Oh, fuck me."

Benedict, beautiful, brazen Benedict, lets out a warm, mocking laugh, his hoarfrost eyes practically incandescent with glee. "We've only just met. But if you insist."

Chapter Four

"WE CAN'T."

"We absolutely can."

"We can't have a fae prince sleeping on our sofa."

"But—"

"I don't like fae. No vampire likes fae."

"You know, no one's ever explained to—"

"Because they treat us like second-class citizens. There's—there's a rumor that we're actually the degenerate children of the Redcaps, the mongrel halfling kids of the lowest of the low."

I wince. "Look, just because he's part of the Sidhe Court, it doesn't mean that he's going to be, er, species-ist, or anything like that. It's possible that he might be entirely against that historical tension. Who knows? This might be an opportunity for vampires everywhere! One day, young vampires might point at this moment and say, 'This is how we got justice for all the wrong that was committed against us! This is where one of our ancestors stood up to the fae, and this is where we won equal treatment!'"

Zora pauses, stares, begins counting off her fingers. "Two things. Number one: you have a point. I guess. There is a chance that Benedict's not a complete arsehole. A small chance, but a chance, nonetheless. So, I'll give you that. Grudgingly. Number two: Never, ever use that rhetoric on me unless you're willing to go up to an African-American person and tell them the same thing, okay?"

"I'm not sure if that's even the same—"

"Whatever. My mind's made up. I'm not standing for this. I'm not. You're just going to have to—"

"—let him spirit me off to the Ritz where I'll be vulnerable to his nefarious advances? Who knows what manner of nefarious things—"

"I don't know if you realize, but you're a *Kodiak bear*. You belong to the largest brown bear species in the world! You can bench press *cars*!"

"No, I can't!" It's half-true. I can't bench press your *average* car, but I can lift those cute electric hybrids that Zora's been lusting for. "Besides, he's one of the Sidhe. They've got strange, magical powers."

"You have claws."

"Royal connections."

"You have teeth!"

"Teeth doesn't work against centuries-old sorcery!"

Zora throws her arms up in the air. "There is no scientific reason for you to be afraid of this man!"

"It's the only way he'll let me go to my date."

"Ugh. Don't even—"

"Also, I'd already said yes."

"Double ugh."

"I know."

"I mean, seriously. *Ugh.* Couldn't you at least have brought it up, like, yesterday?" Zora pinches the bridge of her nose, forehead scrunching, before she lets go. "I had *plans*, you know? Plans that didn't involve babysitting that asshole. I had a date with two bisexual firemen planned."

Oh.

"*Ooooooh.*"

"*Bisexual firemen.*" Zora doesn't give me the chance to answer, stomping instead towards our alcohol cabinet. She flings her handbag onto the rug with a clatter of spare change, documents spilling over the thick, green wool. I jog after her, stooping to pick up after the trail of devastation, acutely conscious that our apartment's not exactly five-star accommodations.

There's a pair of knickers, possibly mine, lounging on the dining room table, a—oh, *god*—Hitachi Magic Wand under the sofa, and I think I spot a box of tampons on a bookshelf. You'd think that two women would be better at keeping things tidy.

As I tuck the sheaf of papers into the crook of an elbow, Zora pops the stopper from a gin bottle and takes a long, long swig.

"*Ugh.*"

"You said that already."

She doesn't dignify me with a response. Kicking off her shoes, she vaults over the back of our sofa to sprawl, effortlessly graceful, over the cushions, bottle still in hand. Another gulp. "So, when's Prince Odious coming over?"

I dart a nervous look to the door.

"Merde." Zora spits. "Fils de salope."

"Sorry. I owe you one." The last time I heard Zora curse in French, it was when some middle-aged, New Year revellers spitroasted her car between their SUVs. She downs another shot, then another, another, another. Halfway empties the bottle before I tear it from her grip. Zora snarls at me, baring a sickle of sharp white teeth, and then slouches back, lower lip jutting out.

As though on cue, the door swings open.

Benedict, dressed now in a *different* suit, this one an expensive navy accented by a brocaded pocket square, adjusts his tie. "Wrong time for an entrance?"

I fishmouth helplessly for a minute, before finally finding the words. "*The door was locked.*"

"Indeed it was. A rather mildly inconvenient development, I tell you. Is that really any way to treat a treasured guest, princess? To leave them in the cold like that?" Not an apology. Barely an acknowledgment. Hell, his reply's practically a beratement. Benedict dusts a broad shoulder clean of imaginary lint, before stepping delicately inside, eyebrows raised.

Zora looks like she's about to explode.

"How long is she staying?" He asks.

"Excuse me?"

"That," Benedict seems to savor the word. *That*. Honestly. Who does he even think he is?

"Hey, don't talk about my—"

"As long as I want. This is *my* house, you ugly piece of botany." Zora has all of her fangs out.

"Benedict is only staying two weeks." I say, my voice cracking as I try to talk over the building tension, so thick you'd need an axe to cleave it in half. "Just. Two weeks. It's a matter of interdimensional diplomacy. You two can live with each other for two weeks."

Zora says nothing at first, just stares at Benedict, a small growl rippling in her throat. For a moment, I'm terrified she's going to launch herself at him. But then she stands up and stiffly, silently wobbles back towards her room, both hands raised, middle fingers extended.

She slams the door shut behind her, the wood rattling on its hinges.

Benedict and I exchange looks, his amused, mine embarrassed. He smiles and it's all the warning I'm given before his glamour comes crashing down, two-hundred megatons of magical sex appeal. It hits so hard that I feel the Change roar a challenge, a dull echoing in the marrow.

"Don't *do* that."

"Do what?"

"*That*," I say, licking my lips, trying not to sigh as I sit myself in the armchair opposite, legs drawn primly together. My throat is dry. Inversely, other parts of me are *so* not. I smooth down my skirt, trying my best not to worry at the hems. Despite my best efforts, I'm breathing harder than before and it's becoming a struggle to not squirm under Benedict's scrutiny.

The world bends and warps, honeyed and dangerous.

"I think I'm going to like it here," He announces, his voice pure velvet.

I raise my eyes to see his grin widen further, his gaze lidding. In the warm yellow light of the living room, his irises are practically silver, molten with mischief. I swallow and focus on my breathing.

It's suddenly very, very warm in here.

"I, um."

"You?"

"I—"

Benedict slides back, knees spread, a look of feline contentment slinking onto his face. Still holding eye contact, he deliberately taps the muscular column of his left thigh.

"Sit on my lap."

A nervous laugh escapes my throat. "Excuse me?"

"I want you to sit on my lap."

"Why?"

"Because I told you to."

"I'm too big to—" I rasp.

"You're perfect."

There's something in the way he says it. The words curl around me, a leash around my neck. Spellbound, I slide off the cushion and step forward, a hand stretched. He laces his fingers with mine, scoops an arm around my waist. I feel his palm smooth along my waist, down the side of a hip, where it stops, just above the curve of my ass.

"What a magnificent creature."

"E—excuse me?"

Benedict guides me down on his lap, and I don't stop him. Now, both hands migrate around my waist, infuriatingly close to places I want him to touch, but still oh, so far away. His grip tightens, just a twinge, just enough to make me gasp. If he'd just move an inch lower, if he'd just *squeeze*—

"Did you know that fat was prized in olden days? Girth was associated with fertility, desirability."

"Are you—"

"It made so much more sense than this obsession with heroin chic. Sex is about contact, after all. Grabbing. Clenching. Kissing. *Biting*. Where's the pleasure in gnawing on bones?" He murmurs, walking fingertips up my sternum, careful not to make contact with my breasts.

To my embarrassment, I moan. He chuckles, moving his free arm around me, pulling me forward. I comply eagerly, legs spreading so I can properly straddle him.

"You should take it off." He hooks a finger around the top of my corset.

"No! I'm doing no such thing!"

Benedict raises his metallic eyes. This close, I can see the striations in the crystalline irises, the dusting of creamy blue ringing the pupils. He grins and my breath gets that much shorter.

"Why not? We both know that you're unbearably turned on right now."

"That's not the point—"

"Isn't it? What, pray tell, is the point, then?"

"This is my living room and Zora's—"

"Zora's unlikely to come out here, if she hears your screams of pleasure." He drags his hand up, moving from clavicle to chin, to cup my jaw in his palm. Then, he slides a thumb across my lip, teasingly, as though daring me to bite. "Women these days are all so abominably thin, you know? Twigs and willow wood. No meat to them. Nothing with *heft*. You, though. Oberon, I've missed women like *you*."

Benedict lowers his mouth to the swell of my left breast, grazing the skin with a warm, feathery breath. I don't think I've ever *needed* anyone like this before.

"Do you like me touching you, Zelda?" His breath is hot on my skin, his voice a murmur.

"Yes…"

"Do you like having me between your legs?" At this, he juts his hips upwards, and I moan again in reply. "Would you like me to do more than that, Zelda? Would you like me to kiss you? To put your tit in my mouth? To *fuck* you against this couch?"

"What?"

I look up, surprised, still full of needing, a hollowed space starved for the communion of his cock. Benedict bares a feline grin, every inch the debonair bastard.

"I said: do you want me to fuck you against the couch?"

My libido begins to wither. "I heard you the first time. I—I can't believe you just said that to me, though."

He pulls away, a little bit vexed. "Why not?"

"Because you just glamoured a total stranger? You jackass?!"

"And what's wrong with that? Are you saying you've never had sex on a first date?"

"*This isn't even a first date.*"

I extricate myself from his lap, frowning. The delirium of lust continues ebbing away, leaving me feeling somewhat vulnerable.

"So?"

I gnaw ferociously on a lip, scowling. "So, you've no right."

"As you wish." Benedict's gaze trails to Zora's door, his smile fading to something malignant. "The important thing here is that I hope the tick heard."

That stops me cold. "What?"

"I was talking about Zora, obviously." He flicks his attention back to me, bored. "I want her to know exactly what I think of her peace of mind."

"I-I know, but. I—what exactly did you call her?"

"A *tick.*"

"How could you—"

"Because the *ticks*," he spits the word like a snapped-off tooth, "are a corruption of their former self. Once, their predecessors were Fae. Bloodthirsty Redcaps, but Fae, nonetheless. However, they took it onto themselves to make a new dominion on earth, unfettered by our laws, unguided by our customs. They bled mortals, bled *for* mortals and then mingled their bloods until the ticks emerged, cold-eyed, dead, thin-blooded—"

I slap him. The force of the impact sends his head ricocheting to the side, pale blood geysering from his mouth. He straightens a moment later, dragging the back of his hand over his mouth.

"Ow."

I stare at his fingers. His blood is almost translucent. It shimmers in the light like a dollop of cream from an expensive make-up brand.

"You didn't have to hit me." He says, reproachful, no longer the regal lord, but a petulant kid, stinging from his reprimand.

I ruck my mouth. "You didn't have to be a racist fuck."

Speciesist, I guess, but whatever.

Benedict flashes a rueful smile, as he reaches into his mouth and extracts a bloodied molar. I wince. That wasn't a very good idea, was it? Sixteen hours into my new role, and I'd already caused Benedict more damage than the whole of London. Great job, Zelda. Francesca's definitely giving you a promotion now.

"Do you—"

"No." He rolls onto his feet, an easy motion, and frees the handkerchief from his pocket. Delicately, Benedict then folds the cloth over the tooth, before wedging into a different pocket. "You've helped enough."

I don't quite know what to say, so I sit there, a frown pinching my brows. Luckily, Benedict isn't remotely interested in conversation. He dabs at his mouth with the edge of a sleeve, smooths down his blazer, and then begins walking away.

"Where are you going?"

"To sleep off this tooth ache, obviously. The Fae heal quickly, but not that quickly."

"W-where?"

Benedict sighs gustily, full of disdain and a mild, distracted repulsion. If I hadn't just experienced it, I'd have never guessed he felt any desire for me at all. "Your guest bedroom, which I doubt you have. And since you don't have it, I'm taking your bed."

I work my mouth, but no sound emerges. Finally, my voice seeps through, and it's an undignified whine. "Where am *I* supposed to sleep?"

"The couch, maybe. Or a box. Frankly, I don't give a damn, my dear."

"Wait, did you just quote Clark—"

The door to my bedroom slams shut, leaving me to consider the silence. Wait. No. Scratch that. Before I can even let out a sigh, a thumping, jagged bass begins seeping from under

Zora's door, getting louder and louder, until it rattles the living area like a Metallica concert.

Great.

Chapter Five

"WHAT DO YOU THINK?"

I do a little pirouette, turquoise fabric flaring around my thighs. The drape of it is perfect. It cinches just below my breasts, a twist of gold rope drawing attention to the arc of my hip. An asymmetric cut to the skirt bares just enough thigh to be eye-pleasing, but not salacious. Janine was right; first dress that she picked and it's gorgeous. This is the Batman of dresses, the dress that Zelda McCartney deserves.

"It'd look fabulous, if we got you those gladiator heels and some gold—"

"Wouldn't that be somewhat clichéd, though?" I stare at myself in the mirror, fingers closing over my throat. "I don't know if I want Jake to think that I'm trying to cosplay."

"I suppose you're right." Janine tuts, dissatisfied, as she arranges my hair to cascade along the swoop of a shoulder. This close, I can smell her, white lotus and tea, a subtle sweetness. "We could just go with normal heels instead. Or, maybe, boots. If you want to change up the look."

"Maybe." Her fingers graze my neck. The effect is instantaneous, electric. My breath hitches and my skin warms. I tense as Janine brings up her heavy-lashed gaze up to my mine. We lock eyes, and she jerks back with a tiny eep, hands fisting at her ribs. Her smile is shy, and for a moment, I think about scooping her into my arms, and—

Back up, Zelda.

Friends do not smooch friends.

I think.

More importantly, friends *can't* smooch friends. Especially when they've silently and mutually agreed on platonic distance, and one party's supposed to be smitten with a werewolf.

"So, how did you find out about this place?"

I jolt out of my contemplations, too surprised to say anything at first. "Hzwah—I—what—the who now?"

A giggle, quiet. "How did you find out about this place? It's beautiful."

"Oh! It's run by a cousin of mine."

"Really! Which side?"

"I don't know, really," I sag, relieved at the small talk, the last bastion of the beleaguered British person. Nothing like changing the subject to end an awkward tension. "She's my cousin four times removed, according to mom."

I start babbling about everything I can: how the boutique's personal favorite, the way the owner's been on Timeout London twice already, the fact someone in the the Gothamist allegedly promised to write an article about her, but tragically failed to make that happen, dooming the proprietress to an inability to gain traction in American markets.

Exclusively tailored for plus-sized women, the shop's also got a secret: it's made by shapeshifters for shapeshifters. Technically speaking, at least. Sasha Santiago's blood is so thin, she barely grows a mustache during that time of the month. Nonetheless, thanks to the close-knit nature of our family, she's well aware of the modern werecreature's tribulations, and how best to capitalize on it.

In other words, she's a cold, ruthless, profit-hungry merchant of pretty things who'd rather eat a porcupine whole than give out family discounts. (I'm not bitter, I swear.)

"So, are you going to buy the dress then? I think you should." Janine beams, looping a coil of dark hair around a finger.

"I don't know. Depends on how much it costs—" I mutter, peering about the dress for a price tag. Janine finds it first, a tug on my back revealing that it'd been hiding beyond reach.

"How much does it cost?"

"Let's see—" *Squeak.* That can't be good. When she speaks again, her voice is, quite worryingly, an octave above what it usually is. "A bit."

That definitely can't be good. "How much is a bit?"

"A bit," she repeats, a flicker of hysteria trapped in the words. "Just. A *bit.*"

"Like, 'a month's salary' levels of 'bit,' then?"

"Something like that."

She circles back to my front, an encouraging half-smile on her lips, hope in her eyes. "You could call this an investment in your future!"

"I suppose—"

"It'd be something you can wear, again and again. For birthdays, weddings, special occasions—"

"Because I wouldn't have money to buy anything else?"

"Yes. *That*. God. I'm not making it any better, am I?" Janine groans, clapping her hands over her face, shoulders quivering with laughter.

"You tried." I pat her on back. Lightly. And platonically. Absolutely no unresolved feels there. Nope, none whatsoever. "And that's why you matter!"

"I have an idea!" She says this so quickly, so loudly, that I skitter back, almost yipping in terror. "I—sorry—it's a good idea. A great idea. Does she have a return policy? If so, you could, I don't know, buy it for a night and *then*—"

"I heard that."

We turn to find the proprietress swanning up to us, a valkyrie in varuna. Sasha Santiago is larger than life, larger than fact, with a face to launch a thousand armies, and a figure to inspire entire artistic renaissances. As always, she has her black cigarette holder pinned between her elegantly manicured fingertips. It's technically illegal to smoke indoors in Britain, but that has never stopped women like her. Or Francesca.

"Zelda," She breathes out a ribbon of smoke.

"Sasha."

"So, I understand that you're planning to *borrow* this dress for a night then? And then return it under 'illicit circumstances?'" For reasons no one has been able to decipher, Sasha's the owner of a remarkably *thick* French accent. Ordinarily, this wouldn't be so weird. Paris is only a couple of hours from London, after all. People move, even if their accents stay behind.

But here's the thing: Sasha's not French. She's not even English. She's *American*. In fact, she lived in Wisconsin up till her divorce about five years back. Yet here she is, jabbering like she spent a lifetime suntanning on Parisian balconies. Zora suspects it's an image thing. I wouldn't put it past her.

"No. Of course not. Who do you think I am? I am definitely maybe considering keeping it permanently."

Janine throttles a laugh behind her hand, before retreating behind a rack of last season's discards.

"*Zelda.*"

"Sasha?"

"Don't lie to me," Sasha walks a critical look down my body, expression shading from disapproval to grudging admiration. "You do look fabulous in that dress, though, darling."

"I, um—"

"And I suppose I understand wanting to impress that little morsel over there." A sideway glance, Sasha's smile going absolutely wicked.

I blanch. "We're not dating."

"Not yet. But soon, with the help of my dress, you will–"

"No. Nono. Nonononono. Not in a million years. We're just friends, and she's just here helping me to shop."

The words fade as I peer over Sasha's shoulder, and see Janine staring at me, mouth pinned into a hard line. She heard me. Oh, god. She heard me. I'm going to have to make up for this. For now, though, I squeeze nails into my palms and hold my smile, aware that Sasha's favor is rare and precious. I'll figure out things with Janine later. I will.

"If you're not going to go out with her, who on earth are you—ooh. La. La." Sasha raps a fingertip against my iPhone as I pull out a picture of Jake, thoughtfully delivered to my inbox earlier today. I hate to sound like a braggart, but it's an excellent selfie, if you know what I mean.

"Mm."

I bob my head, lower lip between my teeth. *Mm* is the only appropriate noise here. But the magic of Jake's sculpted abs is short-lived, fizzling out under a surge of worry. I shouldn't be putting things off with Janine. I need to talk to her now. I—

"*Lucky* girl. How long have you been together?"

"How long—no. Oh, no. We're—this is just our first date."

Sasha nods and cups her chin with a lean hand, eyes glittering. After a long string of seconds, she announces: "Fine. You can borrow the dress. But on one condition. You give him my number when it doesn't work out. He looks like the kind of man who can use an older woman's firm, knowing touch."

What do you even say to something like that?

"I—" Another flick of a glance at Janine. "Fine. Anything you want."

"Good. Now, shoo. I've to figure out my own outfit."

"Are you sure you're okay?"

"I'm sure."

"Really sure?"

"I'm—" An exasperated noise. "Okay, I might have been slightly insulted by what you said, but only slightly. You were clearly attempting to negotiate an agreement with that woman. It's fine."

"Janine—"

"I suppose you didn't have to look so sincere about it."

"I—"

"It's fine. Really. Just buy me a pint the next time we're out."

"Are you two going to fuck already?"

We both turn in unison, glare down the aisle at the bum that's propped up against the window. Taking the bus was a mistake. A terrible one. The man leers. To be fair, I'm not one hundred percent sure if he's actually a bum. (Homeless people in London are actually quite nice, and often astonishingly well-kept.) Could be an uncouth backpacker, fresh from a holiday in the Pacific, and still drunk on the idea of white supremacy. Or, maybe, someone with a questionable idea of hygiene.

"Would you *mind*?" I snap.

"No. Not at all."

"That's not what I meant."

"Zelda, don't engage—"

The arse roars a laugh, startling a baby in the next row. The infant hiccups once, twice, a look of surprise etched in the lines of its doughy face, before finally detonating into tears. The mother shoots us a venomous stare, as does the rest of the bus. I glare at the man in the corner, mouthing: look at what you've done. He only brays again.

I breathe in. Calm. I am above all of this. I am a werebear. I am a goddess. I am a woman, large and in charge, a captain who is in control of her ship. This is nothing. I am above *this*. I am above slinging petty insults, and arguing with men who would fetishize a perfectly healthy relationship between two women.

"You're a dick." I growl.

He just laughs harder.

I grit my teeth and try not to think about the fact I can fit his head into my mouth.

"Honestly, it's fine." In the commotion, Janine somehow found her composure, and she wears it like a shield now. She touches a hand to my arm, features strained. The message is clear: I don't want to deal with this.

Feeling helpless, I only smile, hands spasming into fists at my lap, my nerves too frayed for conversation. There is nothing to be done. As the infant's screaming escalates, I hunker down, mind whirring with solutions for a problem I shouldn't have caused.

"So, this is me." Janine jabs a thumb at the stoop, smile awkward. London settles around us like a scarf. The world is quieting, calming, drawing into itself, into the old Victorian houses crammed with too many roommates. The street lamps pick out the gold in Janine's hair, limn her jaw in light. She smiles and my heart forgets a beat.

"Um." I push my tongue against the roof of my mouth, breathe in. "It isn't very late yet, and I was wondering—"

"Yes?"

"I was—I was wondering if you still like Scrabble."

A corner of her mouth lifts. "Sorry?"

"I mean, we could get a pint if you'd prefer. But I figured it might be nice to, I don't know, hang out in your apartment, get something from Deliveroo, and maybe play a game or three. We haven't done that in a while."

Not since we were navigating the murky waters of should-we-shouldn't-we, and thinking about being more than just friends. But I don't say that. Instead, I just smile around my nervousness. London might be a cosmopolitan city, but it's absolutely bollocks at teaching you how to deal with social anxiety.

Janine laughs, softly, every note glimmering silver. "Where did that come from?"

"That dude—"

"It was hardly your fault."

"Yes, it was. I asked you to come with me. If you were somewhere else instead, you wouldn't—"

"Zelda." She closes the gap between us, fingers grazing my forearm. "You're not serious. That had nothing to do with you."

"Look, can we just agree on the fact I'd like to spend more time with you?"

The statement dangles in the air, laden with months of missed opportunities. I tense.

"Even though I beat you at Scrabble every single time?"

"Yes."

We end up ordering too much: two seasonal specials from Pizza Express, Barbacoa beef, chipotle salsa, garlic oil, and excessive cheese; some chicken wings, jalapeno poppers, too many helpings of honeycomb cream slice. Janine's housemate, a wiry vegetarian who fancies herself Cirque de Soleil material, was appalled, and totally no help. Consequently, we made a pact to work on the leftovers tomorrow.

As for Scrabble, Janine beats me, of course: ten games to three. While discussing theories for Westworld, season two. *And* answering text messages from her supervisor. Under that covergirl smile, Janine's practically Professor McGonagall, except she *enjoys* working at Vogue.

"Hey." I lean back into my chair and glare at the board. All night, Janine's been pulling out words like NUMINOUS and

PATHOGENESIS. The best *I* managed was BISCUIT. "You think you'll stay in Vogue?"

"Hm?" Her smile is distracted as she tips cheap white wine into my empty glass.

"You know." I shrug. "Are you planning to stay on? Maybe, move into an editorial role instead? See about climbing the food chain? Or is this just a temporary thing?"

"I don't know." She scrunches her mouth into a moue, a leg drawn up to her chest. Janine rests her chin against her knee. "I haven't decided yet. Depending on whether the scholarship's approved, I might see about going to university somewhere. Get my PhD. The possibilities are endless."

"Well, you'll be amazing. Whatever you decide to do."

"Thanks." The smile widens into something dazzling. "What about you? You planning to stick with the fashion industry?"

"Maybe. I don't know. I—" am a werebear, with a moving van full of related emotional baggage. "I'd at least stay as long as you do."

Whoops.

"Zelda."

Wine-dulled and carb-addled, I slop onto my feet, fingers raking through my hair. "I have to go."

"Zelda. Wait."

Did I just hit on her? I think I might have just hit on her. Gently. Possibly, even gallantly. But I hit on her. And after we've silently agreed to a platonic relationship. Will this result in a trip to human resources? Can this be construed as workplace harassment? "Night. Janine. Um. I can—I'll find my way to the door. Thanks. Good night."

"Zelda, wait!"

Face burning, I stagger out of the door, chased by a cavalcade of uncertain regrets. Tomorrow is going to be awkward.

Surprisingly? It isn't.

I look over Janine's head to where Benedict is standing in the hallway, a hip cocked like a loaded gun. He's nursing a cup of oversweetened Starbucks latte, and there's the barest trimming of a foam mustache over the rim of his upper lip. On any other adult male, it'd look ridiculous, but on him, it's just an endearing failing.

Fae, am I right?

"I am totally serious."

"No."

"Come on," I shake my head free of visions of Benedict half-naked, his shirt crumpled and transparent with sex-sweat, the ridged column of his abdomen bared to the ceiling. "He's hot. What do you have to lose? And *rich*."

"Don't *you* want him for yourself?"

I pause. Do I? We shared a moment, sure, and it was the stuff of wet dreams, but do I *want* him? I mean, I have Jake.

Well, not have *have*, but there's certainly some potential of having fermenting there. More importantly, what is the etiquette of explaining your hierarchy of desires in front of someone you've crushed on for ages?

"Course not. I'm into Jake." I say, at last, not really certain if I believe my own half-lie.

"Are you sure you want to give up the opportunity at going out with a billionaire whatever for a zookeeper?"

"Yes," I say, after a slightly longer pause than before. Was this Janine's way of saying "let's forget about yesterday?" Or Benedict's glamour working on overdrive. It's hard to tell. "At least, I think so. Eye of the beholder and all that, you know? Seriously, though, you should go for it. Even if I wanted to, I've got a proper date tomorrow. Just do your thing, Janine."

"He is—why are you doing this, anyway?"

"Because I was *rotten* to you, and this is the first step in my multi-tiered plan to make it up to you."

Janine stares at me, incredulous. "You're a strange one, Zelda."

"Come on. Just think about it. Wine, fine dining, the opportunity to live a life of leisure on the arm of an attractive bachelor. Sure, it's no guarantee. But this could be your chance at perfect love." I coo, all the while trying to ignore the admonishing voice at the back of my head. Inner Zelda is much too paranoid. I'm not feeding Janine to the wolf. I'm introducing two attractive people to one another. She's a grown-up. It'd be fine.

I am absolutely not doing this to distract her from the awkwardness of the evening before.

"I—okay, even if I am into this. What makes you think he'd be into me?"

"Trust me. You're his type of woman."

"You think?" She smooths long fingers over her stomach, a coil of friendship bracelets clanking in harmony. "You really think so?"

"Swear to god. If circumstances were different, I'd be begging you to elope with me."

In answer, she lets out a shimmery little laugh and nervously winds a lock of hair around her fingers, over and over. "And I could totally see myself saying yes."

Honestly, Janine could probably overthrow the Queen in a week. All she'd need to do is promise the country a regular diet of saucy Snapchat photos. She isn't just beautiful, she's promotional billboard-ready, a gluten-free Helen of Troy for the men of—

Wait. What did she just say?

"You're sure you're okay with this?" Janine interrupts my thoughts, tittering uncomfortable. "Absolutely, positively sure."

"You'll be doing me a favor."

Janine doesn't say anything further, instead turning to undulate up to Benedict. Their chemistry is instantaneous, even majestic to behold. It takes no time at all for their body language to go from salutations to sexual invitation.

But Janine holds her own. When Benedict tries to hook an arm about her slim waist, she twists away, winks at him from under the glimmering, salon-mussed tangle of her hair.

I turn away then, nonplussed, I'm not into Benedict, and I'm definitely not into Janine, who is going to be okay. I'm into Jake. I repeat his name under my breath like a prayer as I shuffle my stack of fresh photocopies into position, and weave back into the main office.

"What's Janine goin' on about then?" Oscar grumbles, looking up as I pass by. I glance at his screen. He's gone and inflated the breasts, lightened the bronze skin, added a whiff of gold to the model's ash-brown locks.

What an arsehole. I make a note to ping his handler, see what she thinks of his covert alterations. We've been making a push for diversity, largely because it *finally* occurred to the the higher-ups that it's actually profitable to cater to a larger audience, instead of just the usual suspects.

The other reason is because our new managing editor, Liz, is completely badass, and I want to see her go medieval on his rubbish.

"Just meeting and greeting," I drawl in reply, thumbing out a message to Liz.

Oscar is being a dick. Xx

"That how she says hello?" Oscar rucks his brow. "Blimey. I hope she's going to make this into an office-wide tradition."

"Just shut up, Oscar." I roll my eyes and slump into my chair in the opposite cubicle.

My phone beeps.

What now?

I twitch my mouth. This isn't the first time that Oscar's gotten into trouble with Liz. Last week, he got an earful for trying to touch a singer's hair. Her *hair*. Said it was because he'd never seen an afro so large. The truth is that I think he'd have been sacked ages ago, except that he's best friends with the chief financial officer's ex-wife's godson, or something ridiculous like that.

As I log into all my social media accounts, notifications popping up everywhere, I slide a glance over at Oscar. He looks uglier than I remember. Squatter. Like some fairy godmother was going to turn a toad into a human, but got bored halfway.

"What you looking at?"

I jolt back into the moment, after realizing Oscar caught me staring, a shit-eating grin fastened on his maw. "I—"

"I'm not doing anything tonight, in case you were—"

A laugh bubbles out. "I'd rather shoot myself."

"That's not what you said last—"

"That was because I hadn't seen how small your prick was yet."

The office hushes. That came out really, really loud. Oscar raises his eyebrows as far as as they can go, skin already an ugly pink. He clambers onto his feet.

"What's that?"

"I'm making a penis joke at your expense." I feel the Change jostle under my skin as I stand up, a junkyard dog stirring in the dead of the night. Muscles clench and bones knit, pushing me towards a more combat-ready form. "What are you going to do about it?"

"Why are you two acting like a pair of gunslingers at high noon?"

We both turn around. Liz arrives with a whisper of silk, an aquamarine dress clinging to her golden frame, a desperate lover who just won't let go. She's absolutely stunning, Afro-punk princess gone haute couture, big hair and elfin features, arm muscles like Michelle Obama. According to rumor, a teenage Liz turned down a barrage of modelling contracts, wanting instead to focus on her higher education.

It was certainly the right decision. At twenty-six, she's one of the youngest managing editors that Vogue's ever taken on.

"Oscar's being a dick."

He glares at me. "She's the one causing a scene."

Liz flicks her cool, dark stare at Oscar's monitor. "And what are *you* doing?"

Instantly, the churlishness slips from Oscar's face, like a light winking off. He narrows his eyes, mouth pinching. "Doin' up the piece like y'asked."

"Try whitewashing."

"Oh, like you're one to talk, Miss Middle-Class—"Oscar looks about ready to jump the divider. I tense, eager for the conflict. Talons push against my fingertips.

"Okay, enough. Both of you! No more mud-slinging, no more name-calling, no more anything. This is a place of work." Liz raises her hands, a frown chiselled into her smooth brow. "That said, I'd like to see you in my office, Oscar. *Preferably* with Powerpoint slides explaining each fucking stage of the thought process that led to this shit."

"Yes, ma'am."

And that's it. Just like that, it's over. Liz turns and sashays off, the very image of a cosmopolitan empress. Oscar doesn't make eye contact, just sinks down and begins pecking at his keyboard, gurgling curses the whole way. I follow suit, sliding back into my chair, careful not to make eye contact with anyone.

In stops and starts, the office resumes operation: a clatter of typing, a hum of gossip, an occasional bloop and beep from the Candy Crush addicts, all the comforting noises of people at work.

After some rifling through Facebook and a bit of good-natured stalking, I pull out a spreadsheet of expenses, and dive into the gory task of calculating who spent how much on what party last month. You'd think that working at Vogue would be more glamorous but nah, not yet.

As I dig into the numbers, my mind expands with dreams of high profile photoshoots. I'd be the only woman there, but I'd be more competent than anyone else, full of ideas for dynamic shots that don't involve the subject being ruthlessly objectified. And of course, Chloe Moretz will then come over to ask me to hang out for a coffee because of that, and I'd say—

Fizzy laughter breaks through my daydreams. I look up from my screen to see Benedict and Janine waltzing down the corridor, looking like they're a hair's breadth from jumping each other. To my surprise, Benedict actually looks... *charmed*. As though the steel of Janine's will is a novelty. (Probably is.)

Before I can overthink my emotional reaction, something else snags my attention: the sound of my phone bursting into the chorus of Bohemian Rhapsody, just loudly enough to make a few heads turn. I yank it out, squeaking apologies, and press it to my ear.

"'Ullo?"

"I was just calling to ask if we're still on for the weekend."

"J-Jake!" I stammer, looping a curl of hair around a finger, my voice embarrassingly high-pitched. "How are you? How did you get my number? I—"

"You... gave it to me? Is this a bad time?" Behind him, I can hear the sounds of the zoo, and also a slightly shrill mother begging her son to oh god, not clamber over the fence. "I could call back later."

"No! I mean, no. No. It's fine! It *really* is. I'm, um, just—it's been an interesting morning."

"Well, I see." A twinge of amusement warms his voice. "Really, though, if you're busy, I'm perfectly fine doing something—"

"No!"

"No?"

"No," I smooth a hand through my hair, trembling, all the while fighting to beat my head into the desk. Maybe, Zora was right all along. Maybe, I'm dreadful at this human relationships thing. "I want to see you. All of you."

Fuck.

"All of me?"

I suck in a breath through my teeth. Is there any dignified way out of this? Probably not. I might as well embrace it. Be a goddess, Zelda. Accept your inner goddess. Channel your goddess.

Just do it, Zelda.

Do it like Nike.

Or something.

"Yeah. All of you."

Did *I* just say that? I did. Oh, god. Those were words straight from my mouth. Honestly, how do phone sex operators do it? I barely said anything risqué, and I'm already imploding with gentle embarrassment.

His answer has teeth, a predatory sensuousness that digs into my core. "I see. Well, that can be arranged. Are you still picking me up from my apartment?"

My confident facade immediately melts into low-level anxiety. "Yes? No? Is there a right answer? Haha. That was a silly thing to say, wasn't it?"

A polite silence replies.

"Right. Um, so I was thinking that, maybe, you know, we could meet up in—" I probably should have thought about this beforehand. "—Olive Garden."

"*Olive Garden*?" He asks, about the same time a voice in my head demands an annotated explanation. The most significant date of my twentysomething life, and all I have to offer are the words *Olive Garden*?

I cringe. But then I'm hit by inspiration, or more specifically, a memory of Zora eagerly describing this place that September's boytoy had taken her to. "Actually, how 'bout Bao?"

More silence before he acquiesces, slow and careful. "Sounds lovely. Do you want to meet there, or shall we go together?"

"We'll meet there."

"Perfect. See you soon."

Jake's apparently not one for awkward good-byes. The abruptness isn't enough to leech from my happiness, though. Delicious with excitement, I attach my phone to its charging port, and swivel to find Janine and Benedict standing about a foot behind me, both smiling.

"Hi." I cross my arms.

Benedict doesn't reply, only curls his lip. Janine has finally consented to having him wrap an arm about her shoulders.

"Soooo…" Janine purrs, stroking the back of her fingertips along Benedict's chin. "We were thinking—"

"Yeeeees?"

"Do you want to do a double date?"

"A what?" My jaw slops open, and all the sudden, I'm a goldfish out of water, a cow being led to the slaughter, gaping and gawping and completely out of my element. What's even happening anymore? "You want—wait, what. You—"

"Do you want to go on a double date? Tomorrow? You and me and Benedict—" Janine shrugs, fingers pulled back into an uncertain fist. She's still fighting the glamour, but it looks like she might be losing. "—and whoever."

"Jake. His name is Jake. But, that isn't really relevant, is it?" I grind the next words through my teeth, every syllable spoken very slowly, very deliberately. Hopefully, Janine gets the hint. "Don't you," I look between them, "think that it'd be *better* if you two had some private quality time together? Get to know each other *alone*? *Without* interruptions by another happy couple?"

"No."

"Nope."

Damnit.

Benedict untangles his arm from Janine, his eyes practically phosphorescent. "Really, Zelda, just think about how *useful* a double date could be! You'd be able to fulfill your obligation to my aunt *and* enjoy a beautiful night with two people

who love you, and who can help vet your nascent paramour. Doesn't that sound wonderful?"

I'd rather listen to Zora singing karaoke.

"It sounds *exquisite*." I growl.

"*Goody.* We're all set, then. Just send us the time and venue, and we'll see you there," Benedict scans the office, a lord in his castle. "Why, we could even walk there together!"

Chapter Six

ON A SCALE OF "MASCARA in the eyes" to "apocalyptic destruction of all mankind," today's been about an eight, so far.

Why?

Let's see. So far, I've ripped my new dress (I have no idea to explain to Sasha), had to rush to exchange it for an even frumpier version, wait for Benedict to finish primping, smear my make-up in a localized drizzle, and then go all the way to the center. Of course, the Bakerloo had to be an utter wash too.

Thanks to construction work, everyone's who is anyone in London is on the same bloody, sweltering train as us. And none of them, I can tell you this, are happy with the large woman in their midst.

Discreetly as possible, I mop at my chin. In all the excitement of the last two days, I'm still colossal now, a fact the other commuters don't let me forget as they lean away. Every one in three stops, someone inevitably starts whispering about the virtues of staircases and long walks through a freezing city, and why doesn't the fat chick get up and *leave.*

I roll my eyes.

"Are we there yet?" Benedict grumbles, not for the sixth time. Clearly, he hasn't had to spend much time on the tube. He scowls as he dangles from a rail, waistcoat draped over an arm. His outfit today is surprisingly low key. No thousand-dollar brand names, as far as I can tell. Instead, he's got on an elegant pastiche of stripes and indigo velvet, with the most beautiful two-toned wingtips. "No."

"How about now?"

"No."

"Now?"

"No."

Claws push against the skin of my fingertips. "You sound like a child. If you didn't want to be in the tube, why didn't you spend some of that trust fund to get us a cab?"

He shrugs, elegant despite exhaustion, the only blemish in his impeccable attire being the blue scrunchie he'd borrowed from a massively unhappy Zora. "I was curious."

"Well." I adjust my top. "Deal."

Eventually, we creak to a halt and the doors screech apart. Benedict goes out first, easily wafting through the ropes of people. I'm not quite so limber. I wait until the last commuters have gotten up and meandered to the doors before I power-walk towards escape. There's a science to it. You get a gap of two seconds before the next wave of tired Londoners shamble in. If you make it within two feet of the doors before that happens, they'll slow down to let you through.

Fail, well…

"Excuse me! Ex—could you please let me through—I'm sorry, if you could just move—ouch!"

I escape the crowd with a stubbed toe, elbowed ribs, and a few disparaging comments. Pulling my coat around me, I inch up to Benedict, who is dramatically posed against a pillar.

"What took you so long?"

"Shut up and keep walking."

"Temper!" Benedict chortles, before darting up the steps two at a time. If Francesca wasn't my boss, prince or no prince, I swear I'd throttle his scrawny little neck.

Even if his arse is an impressive view.

We find our way to BAO (spelled with capital letters, I discover, rather than with grammatical accuracy) about half an hour late, both slightly sweaty from effort.

Janine and Jake, on the other hand, look amazing. Jake's in a long-sleeved white shirt, nicely pressed, and distressed grey jeans, with candy-trimmed Adidas superstars for a note of color. Very simple, and almost forgettable if it weren't for the fact it looks like someone'd painted the shirt and jeans on him. Who knew that cloth could cling to oblique muscles like that?

And Janine, well, Janine's basically Jessica Rabbit on her night off: fresh highlights, cream-colored clutch by Louis Vuitton, black sheath dress, cut extraordinarily low, and gladiator heels. Every man in a twenty-feet radius is staring at her, and I don't blame them.

"You look fabulous." I blurt out.

She titters nervously, eyes bright and endearingly vulnerable. "Thanks."

"You do too." To my surprise, Jake turns from Janine to gawk at me, full of naked lust. He strips me with his eyes, carefully, methodically, until I can almost feel the wind pimpling my flesh. My world contracts into a pinpoint of raw, eager desire. "You look better than I remember, really."

Wait. What did he—

But now Jake's got an arm out like a proper gentleman, and there's just no room to be indignant. I loop my fingers around his elbow. He beams down at me, dark curls flopping over his eyes, smile widening. Mine, his posture says. All mine.

"What? No one's going to say how lovely I look?"

I hear Janine's laugh again, slightly forced, and heavy with notes of, "What the hell am I doing?" Instantly, guilt rustles over me, mingling with a flicker of spiteful hope. Is it wrong that I hope this will escalate massively and end with Janine daintily splashing champagne in Benedict's face, before storming out like Scarlett O'Hara at her best.

Probably.

I squash my fantasies and shepherd the group up to BAO, which proves to be positively darling. White wood on the outside, golden warmth on the inside, big glass windows advertising a cluster of eager diners, their tables rife with tiny plates and fluffy artisan buns.

We step in.

A discordant murmur of greeting eddies through the room, before a spritely waitress, laser-cut razor bob accenting the stark red lipstick, bounces in front of us.

"Sorry!" She beams. Her accent's got just enough French in it to make every remark a question. "How many people?"

"Um. Four." I respond.

The waitress nods once, quite sternly, before gesturing at the door, even as she begins to amble forward, arms stretched like the wings of a mother hen, herding us out. "It's about a twenty minute wait. Not too long at all! If you'd go park yourselves across the street, we'll be done."

And just like that, she marches us back into the damp chill, where we then shuffle up behind a pair of well-dressed men, both in matching grey Hugo Boss suits, their hands intertwined.

Benedict's the first one to speak.

"Tell me again why you didn't make reservations."

"Ben!" comes Janine's hushed, scandalized rebuke.

I shrug a shoulder, after glancing at Jake, who has now apparently tuned out the whole mess and is fixated by football statistics. "Because they don't take reservations."

"You sure?"

"Yes."

"*Really* sure?"

Deep breaths, Zel. I slot my hands under my armpits and count to ten, before cocking my head. "Listen, buddy. First off, do you really think I'd rather be in here in the cold, arguing with you, instead of snuggled up inside there? Secondly, you invited yourself to—"

Benedict rolls his eyes and moves his attention to Janine, not even bothering with a comeback. Arse. And then I feel it. The gossamer, glittery presence of his glamour as he extrudes it like a web. The world thickens with it, a lushness, a sultry richness of being that makes every color brighter, more breathtaking, a ring of courtiers surrounding the natural fulcrum of all existence: Benedict.

Except he isn't as handsome as I remember.

Or as deliciously svelte.

Just a little bit pale.

And far too skinny.

And slightly *vegetal*-looking, come to think about it. With pinched features and a mouth like a slit.

He reminds me of those plants mums give their college-going kids, those reedy things that look like they'd survive the bloody apocalypse.

It hits me that my initial attraction to Benedict was probably manufactured, a byproduct of his ambient glamour. Something's thrown him off his game today. Maybe, the weather. Maybe, the hour in the tube. Whatever the case, I'm no longer in his sphere of influence, which means I get to witness Benedict in all of his natural perfection.

Ew.

Horror swells in my breast, subsuming even the pleasure of Jake's renewed focus, his nonsensical compliments. I shoot a meaningful look at him. Can't he *see* what I'm seeing? Doesn't he care?

The expression on his face says no. I clench my teeth and look about. Just yesterday, this would have been my dream come true. To monopolize all of Jake's attention, to have him drooling after me like a prime cut of beef. But right now? Right now, all I want to do is get a giggling, glamour-drunk Janine away from Benedict.

Why can't life be *simple* for a change?

"Your table is ready!"

It doesn't take *too* long to seat us. Note the sarcastic emphasis. BAO was apparently built with straw-thin hipsters in mind, as opposed to anyone possessing your typical British waistline. The waitress ends up playing Tetris with a few patrons, rearranging them to make room for me, all the while apologizing, even as the affected diners glower at my circumference.

But soon, the ordeal is over, and we're all plunked into our chairs at a corner, one big dysfunctional family. I'm squeezed between Benedict and Jake, with Janine sequestered between the wall and everyone's favorite arsehole faerie prince.

"'Bout four and five dishes should do you good. If you've got any questions, let us know!" The waitress flounces away.

I barely pay any attention to the listing. Janine, for all my concern, seems perfectly happy, the vision of flirtatious good will. She picks out the vegetarian options (obviously), while Benedict laments the lack of sophistication. Jake ignores both of them, and shoots straight for the meat-arian options.

"And you, ma'am?"

"What?"

I look around to see the bright wedge of a professional smile. "What's your order?"

"Oh!" I startle, banging my knee against the countertop. When did she get back here? Stammering, I pick out a cluster of dishes.

"Are you sure?"

"Y-yes?"

"*Three* house pickles?"

"Did I say three?" Damnit, I sound like I've swallowed helium. "I meant two. One! Actually, how about you get me your favorites."

Expression betraying mild concern, the waitress bobs her head, and withdraws into the bustle, leaving Jake to stroke my back.

"You okay?"

"Yes." No.

"You look like you've got poachers on your tail."

"It's that—you know. It's that time of month."

Comprehension illuminates Jake's gaze. "Yeah, I know what that's like. It's... hard for me too."

I scan the restaurant, brow rucked. "Really? How so?"

"Appetites." His fingers write lines of fire down my arm as they travel to my hand. My breath catches, hitches. "It's hard to be inside here and not think of everyone else as food."

At that last word, his eyes flash a lurid yellow, just for a second, like a cat's eyes in the headlights of an incoming truck. I stiffen in riposte. It's no secret that werecreatures will occasionally snack on a drunk, but the fact that the compulsion's creeping up on Jake in a crowded restaurant, well, that's not good at all. Especially given that there's also a hungry werebear here.

"Don't you *dare* eat anyone."

Jake laughs breezily. "Please. It's too public. Can't say I'd hold back the claws when we're alone, though. You know, I'm really glad you asked me out tonight."

"R-really?"

He rakes his nails over my skin and I'm abruptly, infuriatingly turned on. Right. I'd pretty much propositioned him at point-black range earlier, hadn't I? This is why I stay home watching Netflix. Because the outside world is a terrible idea.

"Really."

"Why's that?"

"Because I think we might have missed an opportunity. I didn't pay you enough attention in high school."

"Crap. You remember."

"Uh huh."

Something crystallises inside of me. "So, why didn't you ask me out?"

He twitches a muscular shoulder. "Appearances, I suppose. I had a… *type*. A territory to carve out. I had to keep up appearances. Make sure people knew who I was, and what I was capable of."

"And that meant sleeping with all the cheerleaders?"

His smile is dazzling. "All at once."

"And ignoring the fat girl."

"You were big-boned. Not fat."

"No. " I frowned. "I *am* fat. I am large. I am whatever you'd like to call me. Bears aren't built small. I don't think I like how you're—"

"However you'd like to put it. Regardless, you weren't what people would have seen as 'my type.'" He draws circles across my palm, utterly unaware of how his words were lancing through me. "But we can make up for it now, can't we?"

Anger throbs. "We can?"

"Tonight and maybe, every alternate night for the conceivable future. We could have a lot of fun together."

The urge to loathe him is immediate, but Jake's just operating on instinct, isn't he? He's an animal. I'm an animal. It should all be fine.

Except it's not.

"It's—it's a thought. We'll see how the night goes, won't we? Then, maybe, you could come up, um, across the hall and maybe, we could. Talk." I squeeze his arm reassuringly, more out of a lack of inspiration as to what to do next rather than any real urge to offer comfort, even as his eyes widen in confusion.

Really, though, tonight can go cram itself into a bin.

"Janine?" I lean cautiously back and look to Janine, dropping my conversation with Jake like a hot potato. "How are you doing?"

She peers back. "Fine?"

"Like, how fine?"

Janine glances surreptitiously at Benedict, who is suspiciously disinterested in our dialogue. "Very?"

"On a scale of one to ten—"

"I don't see how this has to do with anything."

"Six then?"

Her mouth clacks shut. "Eight?"

"Seven point five?"

"Zel—"

We're interrupted by someone delicately clearing their throat. I look around to see our waitress, platters of food balanced along her arms. Her smile is mildly pained. "Sorry," she says, in a way that suggests she's not sorry, but in fact would rather *I* be sorry.

She sets our orders down, a neat jigsaw of earthen bowls and indigo plates. The smells hits me immediately and despite the knot of worry in my stomach, I'm salivating.

Pork confit, dribbling a piquant sauce. Fried chicken sandwiched between kimchi and Szechuan mayo, practically crackling from the fire still. More sauce-drenched fried chicken. Exquisitely cooked lamb shoulder, dressed in what looks like jalapeno sauce. Miso soup. A mandatory serving of sweet potato chips, drizzled in plum salt.

"And this is your pig's blood cake." The waitress sets a slab of black, atop which has been set a runny blob of golden yolk. "Bon appetit!"

Chapter Seven

"THIS IS ALL YOUR FAULT!"

"What?"

Zora's voice through the phone is tinny, slightly tipsy. In the background, I hear the swirl of laughter and bad EDM, thump-thumping furiously. Someone says something to Zora and she laughs, a fake and glassy sound.

"I said: this is all your fault!" I croak, a finger jabbed into my ear.

"Can't hear you!"

"I should have never agreed to this date—"

"Please. Like you weren't drooling over Jake."

"I was! But it's also the reason I did something awful," I begin pacing the length of the women's bathroom, which is to say I take about two steps, turn around, and repeat. A distant part of my head takes note of the fact it's actually quite nicely appointed for something so small. The sink's even adorned with potpourri. Seven point five. Good job, BAO.

"Pardon, Zelda, but *you* did the something awful. Not me," Zora sniffs, disdainfully, ripping me from my appraisal of the bathroom.

"But you started the ball—oh, fine. You're right. You were always right. I should have told Benedict to bugger off. This double date is a nightmare," I crack open the door to the outside world and look out to see Janine daintily feeding Benedict a sliver of roasted meat, and Jake nonchalantly flirting with a waitress.

"Wait." Zora's voice sharpens. "Double date?"

"Yeah." I reply, distracted by the realization I wasn't terribly jealous. If anything, I'm a bit relieved to see Jake getting interested in someone else. It's like the universe's way of saying I'm not losing points with Mr. Perfect, just Mr. Perfect Abdominal Muscles. "So, I tried to get Benedict off my back by introducing him to Janine because no one can resist Janine. They hit it off and before I know it, they've invited themselves to a double date with Jake and I."

"Why didn't you say no?!"

"Because he's Francesca's nephew," I whine, as I dodge back into the bathroom. "I can't—"

"Yes, you can! Two letters. N and O. Just put them together. Easy! That's all you had to do."

"Anyway," I raise my voice, desperate to get a word in. "Anyway, I realized it was all a mistake and Benedict's actually this hideous tree-thing and he might be using glamour to get his rocks off with Janine, and I don't know what to do."

Silence.

"It's your mess. Dig yourself out of it."

"Zora, please—"

"Merde, what am I supposed to do with you? Ugh. Okay. Try this."

And then she dispenses the most inanely, breathtakingly simple solution anyone could possibly think of.

"What if that doesn't work?"

"Well, you're a motherfucking *werebear*, aren't you?"

I am a werebear.

I *am* a werebear.

I am a mother-*fudging* werebear.

I slam the door to the bathroom, drama thundering in my bones. The wooden panel *whumphs* into the wall, causing, just for a moment, all activity in the restaurant to cease. Everything. Not a whisper, not even the tinkling of silverware scraping over clay, or the telltale bloop of someone Vine-ing my humiliation. Just the stark, awkward silence of the baffled.

"S-sorry. Don't know my own strength. Ahahah. Ha. Ha." Maybe, I should have reconsidered that entrance. Yeah. I definitely should have. I sidle along the wall and then, head bowed, scoot back to my spot between the guys.

"What," Benedict's voice is flat, dry, totally unimpressed. "Was that all about."

"Lay off, man," Jake comes to my rescue, a growl bristling in his voice, before I can even put two syllables together. "It's her time of the month."

I wince. Technically, he's right. I'm, maybe, a week from a full transformation. But did Jake have to say it like that?

"I can fight my own battles, Rover." I flatten a palm against his chest.

This time, Jake actually growls, a perfectly canine noise that causes Janine to startle, dropping her cutlery. Benedict bares needlepoint teeth. Who needs to waggle dicks when you can compare dentures? Benedict flaps a hand and again, his glamour courses through the restaurant, wrapping the room in a buttery fog.

All but the three of us.

As everyone else relaxes into the fugue, Benedict snarls: "Didn't anyone teach you to behave around your betters? Sit. *Pup.* I was old before your kind was even conceived."

Jake launches halfway to his feet. Veins bulge against the skin of his throat and his arms, even as he actually snaps his teeth at Benedict, half-barking in rage.

"SHUT. UP."

That shatters the tension.

Also, the remnants of my dignity but who is keeping track of that, anyway?

Benedict's the first to open his trap: "You're going to need to be more specific."

"Shut *up*, asshole."

"Jake," I rest a placating hand on his wrist.

"He started it—"

"*Enough.*" I clear my throat. "I've had enough. I—there's really no easy way to put it. *I'm rescinding my invitations,* Benedict."

"What?" He goes still and cold.

"Well, they weren't invitations, per se, but a rose by any other color, eh? Regardless, I'm taking it back. Your invitation to stay in my apartment, your invitation to be here, your very presence in my—"

"Wait—"

"Yes, darling?" I smile, full of saccharine venom.

"Wait." Benedict's actually hyperventilating now, his chest hammering. I can see sweat glistening on his forehead. His glamour winks out at intervals, flashing glimpses of his true self, and vignettes of glowy overcompensation, like someone used the Photoshop smudge tool to paint in his skin. "*Wait.*"

Jake makes a quizzical noise and I smile, patting his arm again. "Go take a few minutes outside, will you?"

"But—"

"Go."

The best thing about werewolves? They're all secretly dogs on the inside. A strong word, and you'll have them doing laps around your little finger.

"Yes, miss."

And Jake takes off, leaving me with Benedict and a slightly stupefied Janine, who is inexplicably engrossed in the wall patterns. At least, she's not mired in the drama. Once I'm certain that Jake's out of earshot, I level the bulk of my attention back at Benedict.

"You."

"Wait." He repeats, gulping. No more glamour now, just an emaciated twig of a person, with shoots blossoming between his fingertips.

"I'm not even done. You know what else I'm going to do? I'm going to tell your aunt that you've been abusing your power—"

"You can't."

"Yes, I can."

"But she *hired* you to be my bodyguard."

"Hired's a bit of a strong word, but sure," I wave a hand, then mime for the bill as our waitress whistles past. "Francesca wanted me to look after you, and I wouldn't be doing my job if I didn't tell her you were up to no good."

I grip the countertop and the wood cracks under my hands, even as I continue. "You weren't supposed to enchant regular mortals, were you? There are treaties, aren't there? And you're violating them right now. So, I need you to tell me right now: what's it going to be?"

Benedict stares and stares, looking for all the world like he's preparing to argue, to mount a counter-offense that will flatten me with its loquacity. It doesn't come. Instead, Benedict sags, twisting his waistcoat in his hands.

"Fine. What are your terms?"

I win.

It's snowing when we finally emerge from BAO, small and powdery flakes that will melt as soon as they touch the ground. In a few hours, the snow will either be forgotten, or trampled silt-grey sludge on the streets. Either way, it doesn't matter. For now, it's beautiful.

I walk Janine gingerly out of the door, wrapping both our coats around her shoulders. She trembles under my touch, weak-kneed, underdressed, and still sluggish from the effects of the glamour.

"You're okay," I whisper to her, again and again.

Janine allows a wan smile to flit across her face, before resting her cheek against my shoulder. "Thank you."

I cup her face and smile, breathe in the soft perfume of her. Sometimes, we get the happy endings that we deserve. The negotiations with Benedict were short and brutal. He agreed to free Janine in exchange for directions to London's sleaziest night clubs. I agreed to accompany him to those places, so long as he agreed to pay for the necessary shopping expenses.

As for accommodations, we settled on delaying it to a democratic vote. The three of us—him, Zora and I—will make a joint decision in regards to which overpriced five-star hotel we'll park ourselves in. Personally, I'm jonesing for the Ritz. Benedict can make up for his errors with lobster carpaccio.

"How did it go?"

I raise my head to see Jake trotting down from around an alley, full of puppydog earnestness. Still gorgeous, still inhumanly perfect in physical composition. But somehow, not quite as irresistible as I remember.

"Good." My expression flickers. "Listen, Jake—"

"It's okay. I get it, " He glances at Janine, face shadowed with thought. "Everyone likes variety. When you're in the mood for wilder meats, though? Call me."

That's not quite the reason, but whatever gets him through the day, I suppose. The male ego is a strange and surprisingly fragile organism.

"It's a date." I concede.

Janine stirs again as Jake lopes gracefully away, her lashes frosted with ice. She raises her head, smiles at me through a halo of dark hair.

"What... happened?"

"I'll—I'll tell you. Soon."

She tucks a few strands of hair behind her ear. "Benedict?"

"Gone." Inside, waiting his turn to pay the bill, which is pretty much the same thing.

Janine pinches her mouth into a frown, eyes already regaining their usual clarity. With a muttered curse, she fumbles through her clutch for her glasses. "Weren't you on a date—"

"Yeah. Was. But, you know. It didn't work out."

"So it's just you and me, then?"

"Yeah." My voice grows hoarse. "Janine, I'm—Jesus. I'm sorry. For tonight. For—for everything. I shouldn't have left you with Benedict. He has a way of getting under people's defenses. He—"

"Wasn't your fault."

I swallow. "Yes, it was. I should have kept you away from him."

"Why?"

"I can't tell you." Yet. Not until the glamour has worn off in its entirety, and I can sit her down with a cup of tea and a clean-up crew in preparation. After everything that has happened, she deserves to know. "But I need you to trust me. I'm going to get you home. And—and you're important to me. I know I should have told you before. I've—god, I've been a screw-up. I nearly got you—I owe you so much. I'll explain everything. Right now, all I want is to make sure you get home safe."

"That's very decent of you." Janine moves ever-so-slightly closer, her lips a hair's breadth of mine. I feel her lift onto her toes and instinctively, clasp her waist to steady her.

"Do you—I don't know. Do you want to call an Uber or something, maybe?"

Her breath smells of bacon and sweetness, a bite of jalapenos and the faintest hint of lemonade, a stab of tequila. I can tell what she wants, and I want it too. I want to lose myself myself in the taste of her mouth, kiss her until the air burns from my lungs. But I don't, I don't. I need to tell her everything first, see if she'd rather run away screaming, because after everything that has happened, Janine deserves that choice.

I touch my forehead to hers, breathe in her closeness, memorize the feel of waist between my hands in case it's the last time. "I—" I begin.

"You."

"I—I'm sorry."

"I like you, you know?" It's strange how things can sometimes come together, like the words of a song you've almost forgotten. Suddenly, everything fits, and all you can think is: this was always how it was meant to go.

Even if it still isn't quite right.

"I like you too. A lot."

"I've been hoping you'd ask me out for months."

"I—I—"

"Ask me out."

"Not until you've gotten a good night's sleep and we've had time to talk about… things."

"Ask me out then. Promise me."

"I—okay."

"Whatever you have to tell me, I don't think it could change how I feel about you." Her palm is warm against my cheek.

I close my fingers around hers, close my eyes, and try to smile. "I hope so. I honestly hope you're right."

Spoiler: she totally was.

Acknowledgments

Even from the beginning, I was always writing this for my publishers. The Book Smugglers were a dream publication for me, an indie outfit scaffolded on a vivid love for books. More than anything else, I wanted to be a part of their words, their world. I was in love with the short stories they'd put out. So, when the call for novellas came up, I practically fell over myself to write this. Thank you, Book Smugglers. For just being you.

(And for, you know, actually taking the novella.)

To everyone who was forced to listen as I rambled endlessly about the complexities of these genres, my worries about not getting it right, my slightly demented giggling: thank you.

And thank you to anyone who came into this blind, expecting more horror from my splatterpunk-y self. I bet this wasn't what you were expecting, was it? I'm glad you stayed, though.

Inspirations & Influences

FOR THE LONGEST TIME, CHICK-LIT was my dirty secret.

I discovered Sophie Kinsella in college around the same time that my sister did. I remember coming home and finding a paperback on the sofa with a creamy lemon surface. Its title made me arch a brow. *The Undomestic Goddess*, it said. I'd snickered.

You have to understand that my alma mater was predominantly male. My classes had six girls, maybe eight. Some classes were all testosterone. The college I attended specialized in all things technology, taught only all things technology, and prototypical nerdbros were the status quo. As such, there were very specific ideas of cool. D&D was acceptable, *Gilmore Girls* was not. Video games were divisive: DDR made you effeminate (unless you can also breakdance[1]), turn-based

---

1   https://www.youtube.com/watch?v=4KoEbmghCgE

RPGs perched on the border, and multiplayer extravaganzas like DotA and Counterstrike meant you were the real deal.

And chick-lit? Chick-lit was social suicide.

So, I turned up my nose because that was what I was conditioned to do. Then, I sat down. Then, I decided to flip through the first few pages, just to see how bad it could get. Kinsella's breezy, chatty prose was like nothing I'd read, a mouthful of meringue crumbled with blueberries and cream. The protagonist felt ridiculous, overdramatic. What sort of person runs away from a crucial professional mistake? Who walks into someone's house and then allows themselves to be mistaken for the help? I was appalled, incredulous, mortified at this representation of my gender. Maybe, that's why my peers couldn't help but look askance at the girls. If this was the norm, well, maybe it was wrong.

But I ate up the book, anyway, fascinated by its domesticity, its fantasy of rising bread, of finding love even at your most imperfect. It was all so normal, so *earnest*. Years would pass before I realized why I'd loved it so much and why, despite the judgment of my peers, I would buy up her entire bloody backlist, inhaling her novels like gulps of summer air.

Chick-lit is, at times, what its naysayers describe it to be: a little silly, a little whimsical, full of unwise decisions, improbable joys. It demands that we believe that all a nervous marketing executive might be everything a high-flying CEO could want, that we can be friends with our bosses, that sometimes, everything falls into place and love, that bastard emotion, is all that we need. It is unrealistic, estranged from the cynicism of the real world.

Chick-lit also makes no apologies for women being women, or women being imperfect, or women wanting to take a step back from high-powered careers, to breathe in the country and the idea of being a wife. Good chick-lit doesn't look down on make-up, BFFs forever, vintage clothes, body image issues, and impulse buys. Good chick-lit might make mothers out of their protagonists, but only because they *wanted* to be parents, and not because a grizzled protagonist needed someone to shepherd him through the tragedy of a wife's death.

Most importantly, maybe, good chick-lit is about *women*, not women as tropes, as things to be coveted, things to be pitied.

And with *Bearly a Lady*, which, I guess, is more of a "paranormal rom-com," I wanted to capture some of that. I wanted a story that wasn't moored in the elegiac monstrosity that defines so much of my other writing. I wanted to create something funny, something compassionate. I wanted friendship, bad decisions, muffins, and moaning about a terrible social life.

Because there's a place and time for darkness and grim ruminations, and there's a place and time for bisexual werebears with killer wardrobes and a soft spot for pastries.

About The Author

Cassandra Khaw has written, written about, and been written about in a myriad of press releases. She does social media for Route 59 Games, freelances as a tech and video games journalist, and spends whatever time she has left writing fiction. *Bearly a Lady* is her first foray into romance, comedy, and people-not-dying-horribly. She can found on Twitter at @casskhaw.

AND NOW, A SNEAK PREVIEW FROM

TEMPORARY DUTY ASSIGNMENT

BY A.E. ASH

HE WAS SCREWED. THERE WERE three of them now, leering, circling, threatening.

Caleb grinned at each of the guys in turn. He could taste the blood smearing his teeth but he couldn't bring himself to back down. Caleb knew what they were after. It was the same thing they always wanted.

"Caleb, you've gotta see reason, friend," Steven Chan, the ringleader, shook his head in an infuriating, long-suffering way. "We don't like to make this worse than it is. You're beat. You have to know it."

Two other guys loomed behind Steven, spoiling for a fight but he held them back with a casual flick of his hand.

Steven always set himself up as the "reasonable" one. Not a bad tactic for such a jerk.

Caleb's smile threatened to melt away in response to the bright, pulsing pain in his jaw but he wouldn't let it. Wouldn't let them get the satisfaction of seeing him retreat. Caleb grinned even wider, gaze fixed on Steven.

"That's awfully nice of you, Stevie. I'm not beaten, though—not by a long shot. If you want my rations you're gonna have to work for them. Work like I did."

Steven shrugged. "Fine. I gave you a chance." He wasted no time lunging toward Caleb, his goons a few steps behind him.

Caleb neatly dodged Steven's first attack, and one of the other bullies—Kassem, he remembered vaguely but didn't know the third boy's name—swung too low, too wide to connect.

Not-Kassem didn't get a chance to swing, blocked by his own allies.

Caleb put as much distance between himself and the others as he could, skidding over the smooth, dry dirt of the Victory Colony School recreation yard.

Don't be there when the punch lands, Caleb's father had always said. *Best way to win a fight—don't get hit.*

Caleb had always agreed—there was no shame in being faster, in being smarter. He looked around in time to see Steven bearing down from one side, Not-Kassem trundling over to flank him then—

"What kind of chickenshit fights three against one?"

Caleb slid a quick gaze towards the new voice. He was surprised to notice Steven and the other guys were frozen in their tracks, looks of trepidation on their faces.

A girl stood a few meters away—at least, Caleb was pretty sure she was a she—silhouetted against the afternoon sun. Her

2

low ponytail was crooked and unkempt and she had smears of dirt down one wide cheek.

She wasn't smiling.

Steven seemed to gather himself and addressed the girl, a nasty grin now curling his lips. "Sammy G. This isn't your business. Go back, or I swear I'll write a letter to Gramma Gao and tell her all about what a delicate flower you are these days."

Caleb watched the girl's expression go even stonier.

"Steven Chan. Maybe you should stop or I'll tell Mean Mama Chan that you beat up defenseless girls and steal their ration tickets."

"He's not a girl—" Steven started, darting a look at Caleb then understanding dawned over his face. "Wait. Don't you dare hit her," Steven ordered the other boys.

"Why, what's she gonna do?" Not-Kassem leered. "You think you can pull some kung-fu shit on us, little girl?"

Caleb watched the others carefully, waiting for his moment. They were off guard. They were easy pickings if he timed it just right…

"Dude, that's racist," Steven snarled at his friend. "Plus, she's not little. Look at her. She's a freaking giant."

Not-Kassem shrugged at the same moment Kassem said exactly the wrong thing at exactly the wrong time.

"Whatever, man. I just bet this little shit here feels real good about being rescued by a girl." Kassem had half a second to smirk before Caleb was there to drive a fist into his soft gut then land a quick follow-up box to the left ear.

Kassem roared in pain and fell. Not-Kassem started toward Caleb then thought better of it and lunged for the girl.

Sammy, Steven had called her.

Through the rage-black that bled over Caleb's vision, he watched the girl flip Not-Kassem onto his back with a sickening thud. Steven was standing, doing nothing, his fists clenched in helpless fury. Sam ignored both of them, opting instead to brutally kick Not-Kassem's ribs with one boot-toe.

Steven bolted toward the main building. Kassem and not-Kassem dragged themselves out of out of the dirt and hobbled away as fast as they could, disappearing through the schoolyard gates. Caleb watched the girl catch her breath, her face flushed, freckles livid against brown skin. She turned her frown towards him.

"Why the hell were they doing this to you?"

Caleb laughed dryly. "Why the hell would they not? A week's rations is a pretty sweet deal."

Sam blinked. "Three against one isn't a fair fight," she said, frown deepening.

"What fight is fair?" Caleb replied and realized he was starting to shake as the adrenaline overpowered him—as the pain in his jaw returned with a heart-slamming, knifing fury.

"None of them," Sam said, quieter than before. "I'm Samantha." She didn't offer a hand to shake but her expression softened a little.

"Caleb Estes," he said and stuck out his hand anyway.

She looked at it for a moment before shaking it just as firmly as he'd expected.

Caleb smiled, then winced from the pain that was now radiating from his jaw to the side of his face. "Ow. I mean, thanks, Sam. I don't like to turn down help, ever. Or to not say thanks when I can." He dug in his pockets. "Here, you've earned this."

Sam stared at the scrap of red paper between his forefinger and thumb. He offered it again.

"You're giving me a full day's worth?" Sam's eyes went wider, her confusion wrinkling her brow, bunching her freckles.

"Well, yeah. I mean, my mom just sent a care package so really, I'm good to go." Caleb hadn't missed how loose the girl's heavy work-shirt hung on her lanky arms, how tightly the military surplus belt had been cinched so that the baggy dungarees she wore stayed in place on her high, narrow waist.

She's probably hungrier than all of those assholes put together.

A gust of wind stirred the loose hairs of her ponytail around her face. She smiled, an expression that that brightened her clear brown eyes. "Wow. I—I mean, yeah. Thank you."

She took the ticket so lightly Caleb didn't realize he was holding out a now-empty hand. He was suddenly too aware

5

of his bruised jaw, the dirt that was all over him, probably in his messy hair cut too short to curl. His tongue still tasted like blood.

"I've never seen you around here before. You just start?" He tried not to slur his words, or slobber blood on himself. He mostly succeeded.

"I'm a townie from Bounty—scored high enough on military-track they shipped me here. It's my first week, actually."

"Military, eh? I can see it," Caleb said and studied the girl—her tall, straight bearing. Her serious expression.

She already looked like a soldier.

But right now, she looked uncertain, at war with something. Sam moved closer to Caleb and her voice was husky when she started speaking again. If Caleb hadn't just seen her beat the stupid out of Steven's little gang, he'd have thought she was nervous—even afraid.

"If—if you want, I've got free periods all next week. Maybe we could share this meal ticket—it is yours after all and you obviously aren't a jerk—" she broke off and looked at the ground.

Caleb nodded so enthusiastically his head spun. "Yeah! Yes! I mean, I'd love to, Sam."

Her head snapped up at his reply, her brown eyes warm and intense.

"I mean, I'd love to," he continued, "but I'm not going to be here next week. I'm being transferred to Metro proper.

Passed my exams with top marks—they're sending me away on the science track."

"Oh. That's… congratulations," Sam said, and Caleb didn't miss her disappointment.

He felt it, too—the way-too-big-to-make-sense disappointment. All his life he'd wanted nothing more than to get away from the sunbaked dust-bowl that was Victory seed colony but suddenly, it was a beautiful place. A place where he could have had a strong, tall and kickass freckled friend, where…

Stop it, Caleb. You don't have a choice.

"I'm sorry," he said, and he meant it. "It would have been great to get to know you."

"Yeah. I'm sorry, too. You fight pretty good, you know?" Sam grinned at him, her eyes crinkling. "Watch yourself out there." This time, she offered her hand to him.

Caleb shook it gently, his fingers feeling warm and oddly heavy on hers. "Thank you. You take care, too, Sam. Maybe I'll see you around." He bobbed his head, an awkward nod or what, he didn't know, then walked as fast as he could toward the administration building.

He stopped short and turned around. Caleb saw her still standing there, silhouetted against the yellow sky, looking at the ticket he'd given her.

"Hey," he called out, and jogged back over to her.

Sam watched him, her expression not changing, but her fingers tightened around the scrap of red paper in her hand.

"Maybe we can send letters or something. I've never known a soldier," he said. "You can give me more fighting tips. Help me learn to really lay them out next time."

Sam grinned, and the world was nothing but sun and goodness.

"Yeah, all right," she said.

Caleb dug in his back pocket for the class schedule he always kept and scrawled his name and contact information, then had her write hers on his Mech Engineering homework. "Good. Don't lose this. Maybe I can teach you how to, I don't know, make stink bombs or something."

"That would be greenie," Sam said, and pocketed the meal ticket and his hastily scrawled note. "And, I'm not a soldier yet. I'll let you know when that changes."

"That sounds great," Caleb said. The bell sounded out over the now-empty courtyard. He waved as he walked away, grinning and this time, he didn't feel the pain in his jaw. Samantha Gao was in his life now, and he wasn't going to let her go.

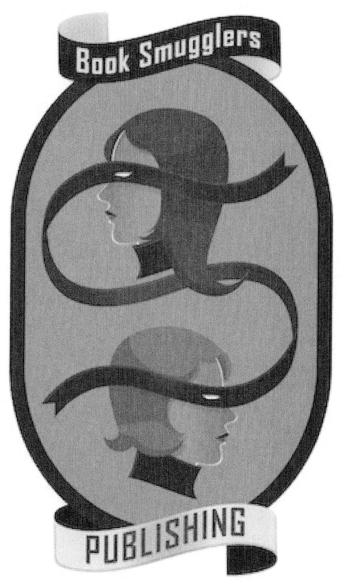

Visit www.booksmugglerspub.com for upcoming short stories, novels, and other publications

CPSIA information can be obtained
at www.ICGtesting.com
Printed in the USA
BVOW06s0235180917
495154BV00013B/105/P